Dreams and Dull Realities

Published by Boann Books and Media LLC

NEW YORK

Dreams and Dull Realities

Stories by John Kearns

Published by Boann Books and Media LLC

For information address:
Boann Books and Media LLC
70 La Salle Street, #19D
New York, NY 10027
www.boannbooksandmedia.com

Dreams and Dull Realities

Published by Boann Books and Media LLC

For information address:
Boann Books and Media LLC
70 La Salle Street, #19D
New York, NY 10027
www.boannbooksandmedia.com

ISBN: 978-0-6151-6636-0
Printed in the United States of America

"Why preyest thou upon the poet's heart,
Vulture whose wings are dull realities?"

From "Sonnet: To Science"
by Edgar Allan Poe

Table of Contents

Flight

Al kinds of birds played in Terrance's back yard. From his perch on a swing, Terry watched the wrens and robins red breast bouncing on the bright green lawn in front of him and poking the earth here and there with their beaks. A funny old blue jay, standing alone, studied the sky before him, above him, and around him with intermittent, small jerks of his head. Black birds sat in the stout trees that shaded the dusty ground on the right. Beyond the trees, pigeons looked regal atop the white, wooden fence. High branches swayed in the lazy, May breeze and two pigeons rode on its shoulders from the fence through the shade to the short, peaceful grass.

The old blue jay leapt and was airborne in an instant. Startled, Terrance trembled and squeezed the swing's chains.

He had come upon a baby blue jay, one time, who had fallen from his nest.

That day a squadron of adults whirled in mad circles above the nestling. Mistaking them for pigeons, Terry charged, waved his arms, and shouted. He liked to scatter pigeons, to see them flutter a safe distance away, and then, once he'd get near again, to see them fly over the fence or into the trees, and to stare up, in admiration, at their flight. This time the birds didn't flee. They weren't even pigeons. Looking down, he saw a little bird who couldn't fly and heard frightened chirps from his tiny beak. The baby blue jay was so cute Terry wanted to help. The bird's mother dove and grabbed the boy's hair in her claws. She flapped her wings frantically as if trying to pull him off of the earth. Timmy from across the street laughed and said Terry looked like an Indian.

The old blue jay disappeared in the branches of the trees.

Terrance hoped the baby bird was all right. Maybe his mother had found a way to pick him up or maybe from watching the big birds circling above him, the baby had learned to fly himself.

Terrance kicked the earth with both feet and swung toward the neighbors' fence behind him. He then threw his legs forward, extending them firmly, and leaned back. He worked hard, pulling his calves and feet under him and straightening up, shooting his legs out and relaxing his back, until he swung high and fast over the fence and his sneakers almost brushed against clouds that drifted in the baby blue sky.

The odd-shaped, cement foundations of the swingset jostled in the dirt as he swooped from the sky to his yard's back fence. A plump robin red breast alighted on a nearby branch, and, with his wings neatly folded behind him, began to tweet a proud, little song.

Mom Mom has a yellow canary bird who chirps like that and like the baby birds in a nest that go cheep, cheep, cheep when they're hungry and the Mommy bird brings them worms to eat. His name is Pete. When he cheeps, it sounds like he's saying his name:

— P e e e e t! P e e e e t! P e e e e t!

He lives in a cage at Mom Mom's house where he chirps and chirps for everybody. Except at night when Mom Mom wants him to be quiet. She puts a cover over his cage to make him sleep. She says, "I don't want to hear a peep out of you, Pete." And she doesn't. He's a good bird.

Terrance had been bad that morning. In the big school, Miss Wick had scolded him during singing practice for the kindergarten graduation.

The boys and girls had been arranged from shortest to tallest in six rows of five students each. At the end of each verse a new child stepped to the front of each line and the child who had been in front moved to the rear. Thus, at the real graduation, every child would be at the front of the stage for a verse.

When Terrance reached the front of his line, the heat from the lights and the turtleneck he wore made him sweat. He stepped forward timidly, feeling bashful and nervous, and when he moved his lips, no sound came out. He knew the words. He knew the tune. He'd sung the song a hundred times but this time his fear struck him mute.

— That boy right there, in the third row, in the green sweater!

Miss Wick pointed at Terrance. Her finger looked pale and cold and wrinkled and her voice sounded that way, too.

— He's not singing! He's just moving his lips!

The chorus came around and Terry's turn ended. His cheeks were burning. Terrance plodded to the back of the line. He had never been so hot in his life.

Why hadn't he been able to force the song out of him? Why had Miss Wick yelled at him? He loved to sing. Just, the song would not come out. That's all.

Terrance quickly forgot the morning's disaster. As he swung up and down and back and forth and up and down, a contentment and a cool, hugging breeze replaced the hurt feelings and the hot shame. He enjoyed this time of the day. After the schoolbus would drop him off at around noon, he'd change into his play clothes. His mother had let him wear shorts today. They were camping shorts with lots of pockets and a shiny clip hanging from the front, which you could hook things on to. It was always nice to put on white socks and sneakers and a loose fitting polo shirt after a long morning at school. He loved hamburgers, too. He'd had one today on white bread with lots of ketchup and a tall, cold glass of milk. From one to three there were no cartoons on, only Bernie Herman and his old black-and-white movies. So, he'd always go outside after lunch, except when it wasn't nice out. Then he'd stay in and color.

He felt elated and free as he soared way up, as his stomach dropped when he swung backwards and down. It was like a roller coaster he had all to himself. He was happy alone. He could do what he wanted. He began to sing without shame.

— Polly the Polliwog!

The tune from rehearsal leapt from his breast, bounced off the back of the house, and mixed with the swish of the wind in his ears. The song made him swing with more strength. He went faster and faster and higher and higher. The ground passed in a blur beneath him. The sun shone pink on his closed eyelids. The chains rattled.

The foundations shook. The simple tune shouted in a little boy's voice. He felt like the birds he'd watched come and go so often, as if he too could take off at whatever time, for whatever reason, and for whatever height he chose.

Mrs. Chimes, the Protestant lady next door whom God had not blessed with children, had told his mother that Terry possessed a beautiful voice. Maybe she was listening now. Maybe she had her ear by the kitchen window and was smiling at the sounds he was making. Just in case, he'd sing with more pride and more energy.

The swingset rattled and shook and squeaked under the strain Terry forced upon it. He wanted to go higher, through the blue of the sky to the clouds even to the moon like the astronauts he'd seen zooming into space on T.V. There was always the countdown.

— ... 10 ... 9 ... 8 ... 7 ... 6 ... 5 ... 4 ... 3 ... 2 ... 1 ...

Then the yellow fire shot out from the bottom of the rocket. The rocket would always rise slowly from the earth.

— Blast off!

In seconds the rocket was hurtling through the blue going up and up and up until it became a fiery dot in the sky like the sun, only smaller and getting farther and farther away on its way to the huge starry blackness of outer space. Then you couldn't see it anymore.

Terrance and his friends would often have contests to see who could jump the farthest off the swing. They would build up momentum as he had done, go as fast and as high as their courage would allow, and then let go. They would fly forward and land with loud stamps a few feet from the lawn. Terrance had never jumped from a swing that was going so fast or so high. No one had, as far as he knew. The wind and his song rumbled in his ears. He was exhilarated every time his stomach dropped. What a thrill it would be to take off, to let go of the chains, to throw his feet forward, and fly, fly farther than anyone he knew, fly like a daredevil, like a hero, like a bird, like an astronaut, to keep going and maybe never touch the ground again, to soar into the blue sky and feel the clouds wash over him, and pass into the vastness and darkness of space! He stopped singing. Instinctively, he waited for the right moment in which to leap, and flew ... His closed eyes saw only a pinkish glow ... His heart pounded ... His stomach felt excitement, fear, and freedom ... and he fell.

He hadn't prepared his feet for the landing. He fell on his knees with a terrible squeal of pain and flopped face forward onto the earth. His mother, hearing the cry, threw down her dishrag and rushed outside with soapsuds still clinging to her hands. Mrs. Chimes hastened to her kitchen window. Terry's mother found her boy wailing and sobbing. His tears were turning the dirt on his face to mud. Blood oozed from the scrape on her baby's knee. Bright red drops ran down his shin and stained the white socks she'd laid out for him.

— Terry! Terry! What happened? Oh, Terry! Don't cry! Mommy's here. It's all right. Don't cry ...

She tried to lift him and comfort him. She tried to wipe away his tears. But Terry's eyes were aflame with rage. He was screaming in hoarse, utter despair. He was pounding a vengent fist into the earth. She tried to cradle him in her arms but Terrance turned away, burying his muddy face in the grass and weeping wildly in bitter, inconsolable grief.

Philadelphia, The Bronx, Staten Island, Manhattan.
Completed Fall 1990.

Dreams and Dull Realities

I.

First, he felt the tickle of the rat's whiskers on the bottom of his foot. Then, the rat's grimy coat slid along his instep. Terrance couldn't budge it: his leg was too heavy. The rat's cold nose probed Terry's heel and the tendon that ran from it. Its paws grasped Terry's ankle as a squirrel holds an acorn. The boy could do nothing but endure it. He had to lie motionless with the rat's hot breath on his calf. Powerless and mute, he could only wait as the creature opened wide its jowls and sank into Terry's flesh its burning fangs.

Vacuous bears and tigers smiled in the corner, where some moonlight fell from the window. Were they happy about his pain and his helplessness? They were just toys. They were for the children, the little ones, who were cooped up, as he was, in the Children's Ward. A cast began at his hip and encased his thigh, his bended knee, his calf, and foot. He had been in an accident at school. The Principal had been to see him today. He hadn't told. The others wouldn't get in trouble. Sister Regina had said he was brave. She and the other sisters were praying for him.

What time is it?

He picked up the small white box that lay at the end of a cord next to him. His thumb pushed down the button to signal for the nurse. He needed a pill for the pain. It did

feel like something was gnawing on his heel. It was awful —
and itchy!

Where's the nurse?

John Caulfield had been pushing the truck across
the floor of the gymnasium. Terrance had ridden,
skateboard style, up front on the right. Other pairs of boys
had been doing the same.

I didn't tell her. They won't get in trouble.

The boys had scooted around the gym on those
trucks and had stacked loud aluminum chairs onto them.
The gym teacher had asked them to. She was nice.
Wrapping an Ace Bandage around his wound, she had said:

— I think you're going to need a stitch. Have you
ever had a stitch?

— Just put a Band-Aid on it. I wanna play
basketball.

That's what they had been doing — playing
basketball — or trying to. With all those chairs in the way, it
hadn't been easy. They'd had to be careful not to let the ball
get loose or it would have clanged on the seats or the backs
of the chairs.

We should've been in the schoolyard but she let us
in early because of the cold.

Joey blew into his folded hands. They were red.
Going inside was his idea. He didn't have any gloves.
Everyone followed him. As usual! Why do they always do
what he says? He's big. He's good at basketball. They think
he's cool.

They hadn't wanted anyone to know that they had
come in early. Each time the ball had threatened a chair

they'd snatched it deftly away. Otherwise, their guilt would have echoed through the corridors of the school.

Nuns have good ears. They say they have eyes in the backs of their heads.

The pain had been terrible when it had happened, when his foot had slipped.

I thought it was a broken leg at first. I never broke a bone before. It hurt so bad I figured that must be what a broken leg feels like. But there was blood. And my sock had a hole in it.

The wound had looked like the socket of a gouged-out eye, bleeding thick blood onto his heel. He hadn't cried, although he had felt himself starting to. Instead, he'd just yelled to John Caulfield:

— Get the teacher! Get the gym teacher!

Where's the nurse?

He signaled for her again.

John hadn't moved right away. During that long moment before he'd acted, it had seemed as if he hadn't understood. Then he'd seemed more shocked than Terry had.

Terrance recalled lowering himself to the floor with great care and slowly moving his injured left leg away from the truck. He was proud of how he had kept his composure. He even remembered pitying Caulfield because the poor kid had had no idea what to do. Some extra strength had come to Terrance in his moment of horror. Some special clarity of mind had let him know what to do. He remembered exactly what this strength and this clarity had felt like and he was glad they had come to him, was certain that someday they would come to him again.

The pain had stopped once the gym teacher had put the bandage on. A circle of students had formed around him. Where had they all come from? Girls had come, too, and Joey and Ed and all kinds of people. They had looked at him, the girls had, with odd but not unpleasant expressions of pity and disgust. The disgust must have been for the blood. Several drops had stained the white tiles at center court. Their color had struck him as strange — more orange than red against the white floor. He'd had a sudden and curious desire to clown for the group surrounding him. He'd wanted to make them laugh, to let them know it didn't hurt, to expose the personality that had remained hidden for the year and a half since he had come to this school. That's why he had joked about the Band-Aid and why, like a kid getting a piggyback, he'd cried, "Wheeeee!" when they had picked him up.

The nurse came over to his bed.

What is it Terrance? What are you doing up?

— I was sleepin' but the pain woke me up. I think I need a pain pill.

She checked her watch.

— Yeah. I think you're right. You're about due for another one.

The nurse hurried away.

For a few moments, at least, a circle of people had stopped what they had been doing and had stood around watching him. He had been like a star or hero or wounded soldier or something like that. He had been funny. Everyone had laughed at his silly remarks. They had enjoyed his humor, his crazy outlook on what they had looked upon as purely frightening. Why, he wondered, had he been required to suffer such a wound, and such pain, and such bleeding in order to create the outburst, to reveal his true self, to destroy his "quiet" reputation, and to begin his life over again?

The nurse returned with a pill and a small, wrinkled, paper cup of water. Terry gratefully swallowed the narcotic.

— Try to get some sleep, now, Terry.

He'd played the comedian all the way to the hospital. He'd do it again when he would return to school. He'd show them he wasn't the shy boy they'd thought he was. He'd strut around like The Fonz on *Happy Days* and the girls would look at him as a hero again ... and always .... from that day forward.

The Emergency Room had not been a place for fooling. Twisting his leg this way and that had been painful. The doctor had told Terrance and his mother that the boy had cut his Achilles tendon in two and that he'd needed to operate. When the doctor had informed him that playing baseball this year had become out of the question, Terrance had finally cried. His mother had cried, too.

— You see, Terry, this is a very serious injury and it's going to take a long time to get better. What we have here is a severing ...

The doctor had gestured with his hands as if something he had held in them had broken.

*   *   *   *

Baseball season had been the time Terry had set aside for the changing of his life. He'd decided to talk more during baseball season, to joke more, to laugh more, to show the kids at school, the girls at school, the real boy that had been hiding in silence.

It was like something burst when he told me. But not all at once. It wasn't that fast. My chin trembled. I tried to hold it back. Then two tears got away. They were hot on my cheeks.

Terrance was a good contact hitter and he had power, too. He almost always got the bat on the ball and hit it hard. In his neighborhood baseball games, he had been counted on for hitting home runs. It had thrilled him to step up to the plate after a few practice swings and to see his opponents' infielders waving the outfielders farther out from his respected bat. In the schoolyard, one of the boys would always pull from the bushes in which it had been hidden the day before a bladeless hockey stick with black tape around one end. With this, a tennis ball, and two teams picked by captains, the boys would have a stickball game going in minutes. Terrance had not inspired the same fear in his opponents in these games, but he had hit for singles and extra base hits often enough for them to be wary of him.

I never thought it would happen. Just put a Band-Aid on it. That's all. It was the shock.

Terrance was a good fielder. He had good hands in both baseball and stickball. He liked to play the Hot Corner, Third Base, where he'd been able to snag ground balls with his exceptional backhand and throw runners out at First from the other side of the infield. He hadn't needed the backhand in stickball but his schoolyard infielding had been very strong. He'd practiced catching high flies for hours and hours. He'd consistently made the catches at home and at school. He'd even made a spectacular one back by the fence draped in red, white, and blue bunting late in the Little League's All Star Game.

That's why it burst. The shock of it. That's why I cried so hard in front of them. That's why my stomach got all wobbly and I had to hide my face.

Terrance had been sure that with these proven talents and the ones yet to be displayed he would have pulled off an impressive feat. He, a Sixth Grader, would have made, he was sure, the Saints Simon and Jude School Junior Varsity Baseball Team. This prestigious position, one which few Sixth Graders ever attained — only one last year and Terry was just as good as he was, if not better — would have given him a stage. No longer would he have been only a formidable schoolyard player and a superb student (which didn't matter to these people, anyway) but he would have been standing, as a recognized athlete, in the school's baseball uniform, in the center of the circle — for a whole season.

Mom tried to calm me down. She couldn't. I couldn't control myself and if I couldn't, she couldn't. What does she know about baseball, anyway?

*   *   *   *

Terrance had severed his Achilles tendon on March 17th. His mother had pushed a "Kiss Me I'm Irish" button across the breakfast table. He'd glared at it, disgusted with the silliness of leprechauns and shamrocks, shillelaghs, and old, bearded bishops chasing snakes around. He'd wanted none of it. He'd refused to wear green at all.

I'm in Sixth Grade now. That stuff's good for little kids but not for me. Doesn't she know how embarrassing that is? It's gay. It's queer. I could never wear it in front of all of those people and let them read it and laugh about it behind my back. I hate when they do that, when those girls whisper behind you and all yih hear is, "Sss … Sss … Sss …" And then they giggle and snort and whisper some more. You never know what they're saying. They're sneaks! Was I supposed to let them do that to me? Was I supposed to let them giggle and whisper and giggle about a stupid button for weeks and weeks and years and years? Was I supposed to suffer all that just 'cause my *mommy* wanted to pin a button on my shirt? Maybe that's why– No. She said she'd know. I couldn't wear it. For Saint Patrick's Day? I don't care. Anyone who asks me to do that doesn't understand. She just doesn't.

His mother had ignored his protest. She'd slid the button past his bowl of Total.

— It's part of your heritage, she had said.

Terrance had held fast.

— I want you to wear this button, she'd repeated.

— No!

— Terrance, I'm going to ask you nicely one more time.

Her teeth had become clenched. A flush had spread over her face. A new tone of voice had given an indomitable force to her words.

— It's Saint Patrick's Day, Terry! You've been wearing green since you were a little boy. Now, will you wear this button to school today?

Still, Terrance had been unwilling to give in.

— I told you my answer and it hasn't changed. The answer is "No" and that's final.

That had been a mistake. His mother had risen.

— How dare you?!

Pin in hand, she'd approached him and clawed the front of his white school shirt.

— Now I'm ordering you to wear this button! Yih hear me? And don't you dare take it off, either! 'Cause I'll know! And you'll be one sorry young man! I'm telling you!

She'd affixed it to the front of his shirt.

Man, she was mad! But, so was I! She was nicer when she came to visit tonight. Maybe she was just doing that in front of Sister. Maybe Sister was just being nice in front of her. Hmmph! And me being nice in front of both of them. I didn't tell. She won't know.

— Say "thank you" to Sister for coming, she said.

I know what to say! Before I get a chance to open my mouth to say it, she tells me! She does that all the time. In front of everybody.

The nurse poked her head through the doorway. She saw Terrance's agitated face and went to him.

— Isn't the pill working?

Annoyed, Terry just looked for a moment.

— It's startin' to.

— All right, the leg should feel better soon. Try to get back to sleep.

She left.

His rage had subsided as he'd waited for the bus and a terror of the passengers had risen in its place. As the black-and-yellow Number 32 had groaned around the corner onto his street, he'd pictured the children in their coats, their schoolbags and lunches resting on their laps or on the floor. Particularly clear had been the vision of Diane Adler and Cathy Richiamo. They'd been in the back, the way back, able to watch him get on and able to see the button. They'd whispered and then they'd laughed.

I know it was under my coat but– Maureen Meehan was waiting for them in the schoolyard. She always does. They woulda told her or she woulda seen it herself. Every morning, she stands there by the door of the bus, shivering, moving her bare legs back and forth to keep warm, hugging herself with her hands pulled inside her sleeves and her hair being blown all around. I'm glad I took it off. Just in time, too.

Terrance had taken his usual seat in the middle of the bus. Bending over, he'd slipped the button into his schoolbag. Whispers and giggles had thundered and screeched from the rear. Each sound had shaken his stomach and chest with sickening tremors. Trying to look natural, he'd pulled out his History book. He'd stared at its pages and had pretended to read. The engine had droned. Still, the girls' hissing, snorting, and squealing had tortured his ears and had seemed to make his whole body wince without stopping.

Only the thudding of horses' hooves and the cries of the Union and Confederate soldiers had been able to block out for brief moments the sound of the chatter behind him. Once Terry had been able to decipher the words in his textbook, the glorious, mysterious gun smoke of the Battle of Gettysburg had drifted across hills of deep green grass. Fifes and drums had driven men in blue and grey to march and to charge, to kill and to die. Bandages stained red had bound wounded heads, arms, and legs.

Bus 32 had limped onto the school grounds and had stopped in the rear parking lot. Terry had let almost all of the others, including Diane Adler and Cathy Richiamo, go in front of him. With a sigh, he'd risen and shuffled toward the door. She had been there, of course. She had stood there waiting in her usual place in her usual posture and seeming in her usual way to be about to burst with gossip. Terrance had not dared to look her in the face. Instead, he'd tried to seem concerned about watching his step. All he had seen had been her knees bending and straightening in the cold and her thighs relaxing and stiffening under her windblown skirt. All he had heard of her news had been a whispered:

— Joey …

*   *   *   *

These memories were starting to tire him. Everything was quiet. It was time to go to sleep. The bed next to his was empty. Maybe someone would be in it when he woke up. He closed his eyes and, then, he remembered the rat. He wondered who played with the silly-looking tigers and bears.

It was really cold in the schoolyard. I wonder how they do that, how they go out there in skirts and nothing on their legs. They say they have it worse than us when it's cold and when it's hot. I can't believe that. We gotta wear pants when it's hot, with sweaty legs and everything. This is still itchy. Try to sleep.

Terry closed his eyes again and relaxed his muscles. Boys bashed into one another and wrestled for rebounds while charging cavalry jumped whirling ropes held by little girls. Footballs and cannonballs shook the air. Children and Confederates played tag with bayonets. Schoolgirls whispered and giggled over the shattered bodies of fallen soldiers.

Terry opened his eyes and carefully sat up. He reached over and took from the table on his right the blue plastic container that was his urinal. He pushed the blanket and sheet away from him and, lifting the hospital gown from his body with his left hand, placed the urinal between his legs with his right. He then had to switch hands. Letting go of the gown, Terrance grabbed the handle of the urinal with his left hand, opened its lid without spilling anything, took his "trigger" into his right hand, and pointed it downward and all the way into the container. Against the sensitive skin, the plastic felt unpleasant, foreign, and hard. He hoped the nurse wouldn't come back while he was doing this.

It was Joey's idea to go inside. He's friendly with the gym lady. He kept blowing into his hands moaning about the cold. I didn't mind it. I coulda stayed out there all day. Why do they always listen to him? Why not me? I should be the leader. Leading us all inside against the rules. Why do they follow? He's cool. That's one thing. But he's dumb. Maybe that's why. Because he's dumb. He's easy to follow. Try not to be so loud! The nurse might hear you. Joey's had girlfriends, too. Maureen and Bernadette and a couple of others. There's always a rumor. Like in the beginning of the year about Great Valley View Swim Club and Maureen.

Something happened there over the summer. Everybody was going, "Valley View, Valley View, Valley View" all the time. Something under water. I still haven't gotten the whole story. The heck with it now! I gotta go and if she hears me, well, that's too bad. Probly First Base. I doubt any more than that. Whatever it was, it was extremely fascinating — I can tell yih that! They always talk about him, always in a low voice like it's a secret. But who cares? Why aren't they interested in me? I'm strong. I'm smart. I'm good, I'm tough, and I'm brave. I've got the leadership qualities. They're all jealous of me. See how much they like him after they realize how dumb he is and he ends up in jail or something! And why shouldn't he have girlfriends? He's only about 43. Dad says he'll probably drive to eighth grade. The blue thing is much warmer now. Be careful. Wouldn't that be great? If yih spilled it?! I'm too smart, too strong, too hotheaded to be one of them. I'm too quiet. That confuses them. They don't know what I'm thinking until I get angry. That scares them. Yeah, they're definitely scared. They can't figure me out. I'm the best in the classroom and the best in the schoolyard but I don't open my mouth. That's why I'm not their leader. They always include me, though, and they always listen when I talk and they always, always give me their respect, but, it seems sorta, I don't know, like, from a distance.

The boys had gone in behind Joey. The gym teacher had come over and interrupted their game.

— Would you guys mind clearin' these chairs outta the way? It'll only take a minute.

Terrance placed the warm urinal back on the table, noticing the odor, disagreeable but not disgusting. He covered himself up with the gown and the sheet and blanket and lay back down. His body grew heavy as he closed his eyes again. The leg wasn't bothering him a bit. Hot air flowed through a vent somewhere. It was a sleepy sound. Spontaneous pictures, more pleasant than before, arose and captured his mind and it went away with them peacefully and without words.

*   *   *   *

II.

A fist pounded on the hollow door not far from where Terrance lay silent and motionless on his left side.

— Terry! It's time to get up, hon'. Terry?

His mother pounded again on the door and Terrance could hear the handle rattling. He rolled over onto his right side.

— C'mon, Terr'. Up and at 'em! I let yih sleep for as long as I could. Now yih have to get up!

He grumbled and shoved his cheek into the pillow. He heard a sigh and then the click of the door opening as his mother entered the room. She placed her hands on his left arm and gently shook him.

— Terry? Terry! You've gotta get up. Yer goin' back today — remember?

She reached over him and with a flick of her wrist, put up the shade. Freed sunshine fell with early light and warmth upon Terrance's face. It brightened the green shingles of the roof, the treeless expanse of the back yard, and the young stalks of corn on the other side of Route 352.

A retreating breeze let the curtain recline against the walls and the window sill. With joy, he began to comprehend what his mother had said. Today, he was going to go back.

— C'mon, Terr'. I let yih sleep for as long as I could. Now–

— O.K., Mom, I'm up.

Terrance sat up and flung aside his sheet and blanket. While his mother went to the desk to get his cane, he studied his thin left leg. It was getting stronger. Terrance took out the cane, put on his slippers, stood, and began heading for the bathroom. As he limped out, his mother removed the school clothes from the door handle and laid them on his bed.

Last night the barbell had hurt his neck and shoulders. The fingers of his upturned hands had fidgeted. He'd been uncomfortable and out of breath. Still, his fingers had grasped the pole, his face had scowled with fiery eyes at his weakness, and, with his toes kept on the board, he had raised his heels from the living room carpet.

— 90 ... 91 ... 92 ...

His aching tendon had tightened, loosened, tightened, loosened. Cool drops of sweat had fallen from under his arms. He'd made his leg get stronger and stronger.

— 95 ... 96 ... 97 ...

He'd closed his eyes hard. He'd come close to the end.

— 99 ... 100 ... Finished!

Like a Gold Medallist, Terrance had hoisted the barbell over his head and smiled. He had stepped off the board and grandly placed the weights back in the grooves they had made in the rug.

Weeks of such work had brought him to this day. Weeks of such determination, such courage, and such discipline had gotten him out of bed. Weeks of such toughness, such suffering, and such refusing to quit had gotten him not only walking but walking on a day of glorious sunshine on his way to a triumph like no other. He'd begun Physical Therapy at Chester County Hospital. The Nurses had understood that he was faster than most when he'd learned to use the crutches with no problem. In those days, he'd had to slide up and down stairs on his behind and use the "blue thing." Before long, the Doctor had cut away the upper half of the cast. His atrophied left thigh had taken him by surprise but it had not remained skinny for long. Terrance had even walked short distances — against Doctor's Orders — with the cast still covering his calf and foot.

None of them woulda been so brave. None of them woulda been so persistent. They woulda stopped when the pain got too bad. They woulda skipped days of training and wasted time moaning and groaning about how it hurt. They woulda whined about the itchiness, the blue thing, about not playing baseball for the first time since they were eight years old. I didn't. I took it all without complaining. Complaining is a waste of energy. It never makes anything better. It's only worse when you say it out loud. It makes you aware of it more and it makes everyone around you annoyed and think you're a baby.

Terrance dried off his hands with the small green towel and pulled his toothbrush from the rack. He had lain face down on the table as the Doctor had used a small round saw to cut the plaster. He'd felt the vibrations and heard the murmur of the machine. Cool air had touched his calf for the first time in weeks. That part hadn't been bad. But then, the Doctor had picked up some scissors and started to snip at the stitches. That part had been weird. Along with some pain, Terrance had felt the skin above his heel loosening as the Doctor had pulled out the pieces of string. Some tears had fallen onto Terrance's cheeks. Afterwards, the Doctor had spoken to his mother and him but Terrance hadn't really listened. He'd been too shocked by the sight of his shrunken lower leg. This had been worse than when he had first seen his thigh. The calf had been so scrawny and pale that he had had trouble recognizing it as his own.

He squeezed some toothpaste onto the brush and noticed in the mirror that he looked wide-awake and full of energy. He started to hum and the lyrics passed by in his head.

> *The men will cheer and the boys will shout,*
> *The ladies, they will all turn out,*
> *And we'll all feel gay …*

They'll notice right away. They'll see that I'm a new person. On the day that I got hurt, I was still the old me, the quiet one. Even during the same lunchtime that I got hurt, I was the old me. But that all changed when I was laying there on the floor with the blood all around. They will see.

The Doctor had recommended that Terry swim to strengthen the leg. Terrance had swum. He had swum every single day in the indoor pool of the Upper Main Line Y. He'd kicked with a kickboard until his arms and armpits had gotten chafed and until neither of his legs had been able to kick anymore.

All this time I've been away they've been thinking about me. They've been thinking about how brave and funny I was the last time they saw me, on Paddy's Day. Every day, they sat there in class and looked at my empty desk and wondered how I was doing and when I'd be coming back. That's what they all wrote on those cards they made for me:

— Get well soon!

— Come back soon!

Well, I'm coming back today and things are gonna be different.

— Bet you'll never forget what day Paddy's Day is on — huh, Terr'?

— Yeah. You'll always remember March 17th — won't yih, Terry?

— That was an awful thing for him to have to go through. I wouldn't wish that on anybody.

Who was that? The relatives. Oh, yeah. On Easter.

— Yih won't forget to wear green either, I'll bet.

— He'll always remember that day, boy. I'm tellin' yih.

Did they know? Did she know? She could have found out somehow, I suppose. The Blessed Mother tells her these things, according to her. I'd be sorry. Anyway, if she knows, yih can be sure she told them. No doubt about it. She's never said anything to me, though.

In addition to his swimming, Terrance had started doing the exercise that had become known in the household as, "heel-ups." At first, he had simply stood flat on the floor and raised himself onto the balls of his feet. He'd repeated this until his sore tendon had started to seem like a tight knot of pain that could never be loosened. Only when he had reached that point had he stopped.

I wonder if they know I'm coming back today. They've probably missed me on the basketball court and during stickball games. I wonder if Sister told them. They'll be expecting me if she did and that'll make them all curious and excited. They'll be distracted.

Later, Terrance had followed the Doctor's advice and placed a board under the balls of his feet when he had done his "heel-ups." This had been difficult and painful for a time but had come, eventually, to feel natural to him.

They won't be able to pay attention in class because they'll wanna know what I've been up to and how I recovered so fast.

Finally, to make the heel-ups more effective, he'd hefted barbells onto his shoulders and had gradually increased the weight. He'd also begun to wear an orthopedic heel in his left sneaker for support. This had taken some time to get used to as well.

I'll tell 'em all about it during recess. If she didn't tell them, then they'll be surprised and that will be even better.

Terrance thrust his arms out and his thumbs up and, in imitation of The Fonz, growled:

— Heeeeeey!

*   *   *   **

What will I do?

I'll start when I get on the bus. I'll get on with my cane and everyone will look up at me. That'll give me a chance to give 'em a sign of how much I've changed. I'll smile at 'em and look 'em all in the eye. Then I'll go to my seat — real slow. I'll be cool. I'll show 'em the new confidence.

Then what?

I'll wait for 'em to come up to me in the schoolyard. I won't have to wait long. Somebody'll come over first, like Jim:

— Yo, Terr'. I didn't know you were comin' back today. How yih doin'?

— I thought I'd surprise everybody. I know how nobody could stand bein' in school without me.

Then he'll laugh. So'll I. He'll laugh like he always does — like he's gonna cough or somethin'. Maybe I'll say that.

— Are you all right? You sound like yer gonna cough or somethin'.

He'll go:

— Am *I* all right?

And he'll shake his head:

— That's what I was gonna ask you!

— I'm all right. I've been workin' out a lot. The Doctor said I got better a lot faster than he thought I would.

— Really! The day yih got hurt, we didn't think you'd ever come back. Sister told us you were O.K. but I didn't expect to see you this soon.

— It's strange havin' to get up and go out to school. I'm used to rollin' outta bed and waitin' for the tutor to show up.

— You had a tutor? Man, that sounds cool. I bet she was like, "I wanna tell you about some Sixth grade stuff" an' you were like, "What do you mean? I'm already finished the Eighth grade stuff."

— She kept me pretty busy.

Some girls will come up, too. After Jim, and Rob, and Ed and Joey, some girls — maybe Megan, and who knows who else? ... maybe Patty or Sue ... — will crowd around when they see my cane and my leg and how I can walk. They won't be able to believe it. I'll give 'em crazy answers to their questions. I'll stand straight and tall, playing it cool, barely smiling. I'll drive 'em crazy with my jokes and Colleen will giggle and grab her stomach like she does and Bernadette will bend over laughing and Maureen will lose her balance and bump into me and Diane will smack her on the arm for almost knocking me over but I'll be all right. They'll want to be real careful about my leg and they'll want to make sure I'm O.K. When they get all out of breath and start to get impatient for a real answer, then I'll be kind and gentle and tell 'em what they wanna know. I'll show them how nice I am and how I don't want to tease them but I want to treat them like a gentleman.

Terrance removed the orthopedic heel from his left sneaker and slid it into his school shoe. He got into his shoes and bent over carefully to tie their laces.

The Nuns'll be happy I'm back. The room won't be so quiet when they ask the tough questions — like when there's a hard word to sound out and no one wants to sound it out or no one can. I hate that when no one knows the answer and they just wait and wait. The time goes by so slow and yih can almost hear the clock ticking from the other side of the room.

Terrance raised the knot of his tie to his neck and patted his right back pocket to make sure his wallet was there. It was. He then remembered his comb. He slid it in with his wallet and, taking up his cane but forgetting his schoolbag, he headed for the stairs.

— We're glad yer back, man, Joey'll say. Reading class was so boring. You weren't there to ask all yer questions and get her off the subject.

— Yeah, and I failed all my spelling tests while you were gone, Ed'll say.

The girls will butt in. Veronica Kelly:

— We thought maybe you'd never walk again. There was so much blood!

— How did you get better so fast? It seems almost like nothing happened to you at all, Patty will say.

I'll tell her about the therapy and the exercises. Sue will suck in:

— FFFF! That musta hurt! Does it hurt now?

— Does it hurt a lot still? Colleen'll say, and Bernadette'll go:

— I can't believe yer not on crutches!

— God! Yer a lot braver than I am. I know that! I wouldn't a done those exercises! I'd probly be outta school 'til next year! Diane'll say.

Everyone will laugh, including me, and Megan will turn and ask me nicely:

— Will it be all better soon?

Then Maureen'll come over. She'll still be laughing.

— How do you use that thing, anyway? Can I see your cane? Can I try it? Please? ... Please? She'll say, trying to pull the cane out of my hand. But, she'll just be teasing.

At the foot of the stairs, with her hands on her hips, stood his mother peering anxiously up at his methodical descent. Terrance, sliding his right hand down the railing and leaning on the cane in his left hand, looked down at her after every other step, tried not to glare at her, and struggled to keep inside him his embarrassment and anger at the mothering she was doing with her attitude and her eyes. The Doctor was sending him back to school today. Certainly, he knew what he was doing. Surely, Terrance could handle stairs by now. How did she think he was going to get to his second floor classroom, anyway — fly? He reached the landing. He'd made it. He'd kept his feelings to himself.

— Y'all right, Terr'?

— Yeah. I'm O.K. But yih know what? I left my schoolbag upstairs.

Terry sighed and turned to go back up. His mother stopped him.

— No, I'll go get it. You go to the kitchen and have yer breakfast.

— Thanks, Mom.

Terry moved slowly, still unaccustomed to having to hurry for the bus. He traced the lines on the linoleum floor with his sleepy eyes and felt happy to be alone again, if only for a moment or two. The tiles were brown with black lines and yellow or maybe gold lines. He wasn't sure. He'd call them gold. He might as well. The tiles turned white as he reached the kitchen.

… home again,
Hurrah! Hurrah!

In his chair, he stretched and yawned and fought sleepiness with several long blinks of his eyelids. He saw the mild and seemingly motionless light of the morning sun through the window with the white frill curtains over the sink. He picked up his spoon. He didn't have any milk.

Terrance bristled at the sound of soft, hollow thuds on the carpeted stairs. She was coming back. The fury that had dissipated moments before now returned, increased. He heard her footsteps falling and shishing on the foyer floor. He put his spoon down and tried to think of something nice.

— How is– Oh! Lemmee get yih some milk, hon.

He said nothing.

She shished over and took the thick-glass, gallon bottle from the refrigerator.

— How's the leg feel?

— Fine.

Using both of her arms, she poured the milk into Terrance's bowl. He spooned some Total, some milk, and a slice of peach into his mouth. He felt better.

— How is it?

— Good.

— Glad to be goin' back?

He hesitated, swallowing with difficulty.

— Mmmm hmmm, he said.

*　　　　　*　　　　　*　　　　　*

Mrs. Tanner was nice. She was different — a public school teacher and a Protestant — but she was good to me and taught me a lot. She gave me that book about the Flyers and wrote a nice note inside saying good luck and how bright I am and how I have a great future. I'll miss that schedule — when she would come at ten o'clock and work straight through all the different subjects without a break and the room would smell like her the whole time and even after she left, a Prod smell, maybe from different makeup or something, and then I could relax for a while in front of the T.V. watching *Happy Days*. Then lunch. Then outside reading or studying on the porch until the others came home. I shouldn't think about all this. It gives me that sad feeling in my stomach like at the end of a vacation. Every time I have to go back after Christmas or after the summer or even after Easter I get that feeling and it keeps me awake the night before. Last night was fine, though. I'm glad to be going back this time.

The bus would not arrive for a few more minutes. His mother had overcompensated for Terry's sluggishness and had sent him out too early. Terrance could hear faint honks from the geese on the other side of 352. He turned to face the flat openness of his backyard and to listen to the sad and plaintive calls. He mused for a moment about when he had seen them flying in their V formation away from the coming winter. Their honking brought back these memories as well as those of the recent warm afternoons he'd spent taking pictures of his neighborhood friends playing on the new grass. He was sorry he hadn't gotten a picture of the geese's return but he had certainly taken enough pictures.

He had photos of his friends running and jumping, making faces and laughing, and even in poses. He'd tried to pose Steve as if he were sliding into second base, but it had come out looking awkward and phony, far different than the way he had imagined and hoped.

Mrs. Tanner had moved quickly, much more quickly than Terry had ever moved through subject matter in school. She had asked him tough questions and given him quizzes, a lot of them. It'd been strange and scary being the only one in class. He'd had no heads to hide behind and if he hadn't known the answer to a question he'd had to say so, which wasn't like regular school at all. He had prepared himself for the day's lesson as he had always done, had done all his homework, and had answered the questions she had put to him. However, there had been some days, some guilty days that had come after spectacular spring afternoons on which Terrance had spent too much time watching his friends and taking pictures and on which he had not gotten as much done as he should have, and, as he stood in the driveway waiting for the bus, he not only remembered but experienced all over again the shame of not being properly prepared.

In general, however, Terrance had remained in step with his tutor. Perhaps he had even spurred her on at times. If Terrance hadn't had anyone to hide behind when he'd been ill prepared, then he'd also not had anyone to hold him back when he had been at his best. Nothing had slowed him down except his own sloughing off and the occasions of this had been few and infrequent. Without a doubt, Terrance had achieved more with his tutor than his friends had at school. It was even likely that he'd done more than those who could claim to be competitive with him.

They had the others to hold them back. Besides, those fruits have spines made of Jell-O. Michael and David! What faggots! They can't compete with me. Imagine a head-to-head, full-throttle competition without the slow kids holding us back. They'd be blown away. The fairies wouldn't stand a chance. They're so gay, they'd rather swish around and talk to all the girls. They'd be like:

— Thay, thlow down. We don't like going tho fatht.

Academics belonged to Terrance. Turning back toward the house, Terrance looked up fondly at his basketball court. He hadn't been able to play any sports in a long time but he'd had fun watching and taking pictures and was in good shape from all the swimming and exercises, too. He had amazed the Doctor with the speed and thoroughness of his recovery and he wasn't close to being finished yet.

Athletics would belong to him again, soon enough. Robbed of that for the time being, he'd assert himself in a different way and become, as soon as the bus arrived, the funniest, most personable kid in the Sixth grade.

The leadership of the boys was his right. With his brains and with all of his talents, there should never have been any question about it. However, if Terrance could combine all of that, today, with his toughness — proven now beyond the slightest hint of a doubt — and with the revelation of his new personality, he would be positively unstoppable. His right to lead would be incontestable. Terrance had earned it. He had purchased it with his pain and with his blood. He had shown — with his drive to come back and not just come back in the same old way but in a new glorified way such as they had never seen or imagined before — that he belonged at the helm and that Joey and all the others should take as gospel any of the smallest suggestions he might make. Joey would naturally step aside because he would know in his heart that he would never be able to suffer what Terrance had and return from it. His inferiority would become clear to him when he would come to know the shame of seeing someone smarter, wittier, stronger, and younger than he is undergo without complaint what he himself could not have endured.

I won't fight him even though they might want me to. They have before. But if he tries anything I'll clobber him like he deserves to be, the forty-three-year-old flunkie. The idiot! He's got a great career ahead of him on the penitentiary basketball team. Maybe he'll learn to read by the time he's ready to retire. I won't fight him, though, just to put on a show for them. But if he provokes me! Hah! I'll break his thick skull for him! Even with this weak leg. I'll smash him in his senior-citizen face, if he doesn't watch himself! But I won't fight him just for the heck of it. He's my friend after all. That's what I told those guys before. So what if they're disappointed? Them and their bloodthirsty girlfriends.

Terrance rubbed his nose with his right index finger. He was glad he had given that up. It struck him as funny that he seemed to pick his nose only when he was in odd-numbered grades. This time he'd quit for good. He would never go back to it. He shoved his hand deep in his pants' pocket. He could feel the flap on the front of his underwear, the weird loose skin, and the movement of the little ball. That was a bad habit he had gotten into. The kids in Little League called it, "pocketball." He would have to knock that off, too. Terrance sighed and looked for the bus. Not yet. He kicked a pebble past the white skid mark made by somebody's skateboard and hummed to himself:

— *... home again,*
Hurrah! Hurrah!

On the other side of 352, the sun was well on its way up. Terry watched a bird fly past it. Another one twittered somewhere behind him. Terrance took in a deep, deep breath and let it out with great pride over all the realizations and recollections he'd had about his life. He thanked God for his recovery, for the strength the Lord had given him, and for the wonderful days he'd had recuperating. But, mostly, he thanked God for this triumphant morning, for the spring sun glowing boldly over the fresh young stalks of corn, for the pleasant breeze brushing their green leaves, for the blue sky and the cottonball clouds under which he would return to such glory, honor, welcome, praise, and popularity. He was very grateful. His body gloried in strength and readiness. God had made this day for him.

While in the middle of his prayer, Terrance heard the bus roaring down 352 toward his street, though he could not see it. It was Bus 32. There was no mistaking it.

Please, God ...

He made a move as if to run away but that was impossible. For an instant, he longed to forget the whole thing and go back inside to his couch, his "blue thing," his T.V., his tutor, and his mother. Whispers and giggles and snorts came from his memory to torture him.

Bus 32 turned the corner and appeared to be coming straight at him.

Please, God ...

His mind raced and his stomach nearly crippled him with its tremors of panic.

— Sss ... Sss ... Sss...

Not since St. Patrick's Day. Kiss me. I'm Irish. Maybe that was– No. It's O.K. Calm down.

The Bus slowed down and stopped at his driveway. It opened its doors for him.

Please ...

Looking down, he thought his aluminum cane gleamed like a brave sword. He went to board the bus.

— Sss... Sss ... Sss ...

Not now. When we get to the schoolyard. Then we'll start. It doesn't matter. Nobody's on the bus, anyway. When we get there. When we get there. Better study History.

He took his usual seat in the middle of the bus.

     *   *   *   *

Fffff ... lllll ... PP! From the window behind her. She's got a sky-blue cloak over her long white robe. It covers up her hair. She's got a golden brooch fastened just below her neck.

— ... be thy name
    Thy kingdom come
    Thy will ...

Fffff ... lllll ... The curtains against the walls, against the sill. PP! Sunbeams, lots of 'em, streaming in straight as strong as spears. She's young, like our age. Maybe a little older. She's busy doing homework. No, sewing. Lllll ... PP! Is she like Bernadette? Kind of but not as dark and without the hairy arms. More like Megan — not too skinny, not too fat — sweet. Fffff ... lllll ... PP! Then a real loud one: FLAP! She turns around. She's scared but she's ready. She sees a face forming ... a nose, a chin, lips ... in the sunbeams ... some long blonde hair like yellow yellow sunlight ... eyes, ears ... a shiny white robe brighter than anything and she falls trembling yet faithful on her knees with her head bowed and her eyes closed before the Angel Gabriel.

Terrance let his lazy eyes wander from the Palmer-Method S, T, U, and V to the silver crucifix on Sister's blue-black chest to the white petals of the dogwood tree outside the window. They stopped where Bernadette Falcone's blouse rose from her ribcage, seeming to promise something still mysterious. They moved with an effort to Ed's blubbery back and scraggly hair, paused to study the dirty, flattened gum on Colleen Hughes's saddle shoe and returned, finally, to the tiny wrinkles on the interlaced fingers of his own folded hands.

— Blessed ar' thou among women
And blessed is the Fruit
Of thywomb *Jee*-sus ...

The heads of the students nodded up and down as quickly as eyelids blinking. Terrance sat moving his lips to the words of the prayer, but allowing very little sound to come out of his mouth. Unconsciously, and, so slightly that no one would notice, Terrance raised the forefinger of his left hand.

The skin between his left thumb and forefinger looked rougher and more chafed than the same area of skin on his right hand. That was because he had been off the crutches for a while, Terrance figured, and because he held the cane with his left hand. His right had had time to heal.

Nice goin', Terr'. You were supposed to start on the bus but all yih did was sit down. You were supposed to perform for a crowd in the schoolyard. But what did yih do? Nothing! Now here you are in the room — in the back of the room away from everybody else and next to this fairy, Blaine — with class about to start! Sister'll probly make a big fuss and everyone will be gawkin' at yih. You can't very well perform now — can yih? Way to go, Terrance. Way to show 'em the new you. Well, what was I supposed to do? There was nobody on the bus and most of the people got to the schoolyard late. The buses were messed up. And what was I supposed to do with the rest of 'em — chase 'em around on one foot? I couldn't very well do that, now — could I? Some of 'em were playing basketball and I was watchin', anyway. Well, all I know is that you blew it. You said you were gonna start on the bus and yih didn't. But the day's not over yet. I can do it at recess. Recess?! Hah! If yih didn't do it before, how can yih expect to do it at recess? I mean, really! You blew it, man. Face it: yih blew it. You planned to do it, you said you would do it, and yih didn't do it. Instead, we had Brownie Michael, the limpwristed Gayboy! Him carrying our bookbag into school! And down the hall and into the classroom! Some triumphant entrance! What happened to The Fonz and the crowds of chicks? What happened to the whole Sixth grade at yer feet? What happened to all yer jokes and yer cool? It didn't happen —

did it? Did yih do anything yih were supposed to do? No, you just came limping in the backdoor, behind the gayest kid in the school — behind a kid even his fellow faggots don't like — and yih just took yer seat with yer chin on yer chest like there was somethin' the matter with yih and yih didn't say a word to anybody. What's wrong with you? Yer outta yer mind — you know that? You're out of your mind.

Was some of his hair sticking up in the back? That was almost as embarrassing as being caught with your fly open. The tickling of it in the room's slight breeze was nagging him to pat it down. Was he just imagining things? He couldn't tell. There was nothing, however, that he could do about it at the moment. He had to wait unto the prayer was over.

They had decorated the room while Terrance had been gone. A white statue of Mary, surrounded by flowers, stood on top of the bookcase by the front door. Above the blackboard, they had tacked cardboard capital letters into the cork. They read:

— MARY, QUEEN OF HEAVEN

Regal and glorious among all those happy souls, her face, her clothes, her whole body glowed like the angel in the sunbeams. Wisps of clouds arose from beneath her and vanished around her veil. She was up on her throne looking kindly down at her friends all lined up to see her, the saints and the other faithful departed, the wealthy and the famous together with the poor and the unknown, from every race and from every country on the globe, wearing turbans and skirts and robes and suits and powdered wigs and shamrocks pinned to frayed lapels. She even laughed once in a while.

Ed sounds like he's snoring. Is he asleep? Yih never know with him. He hasn't changed much. That's for sure. He's still as fat as ever and he still can't pay attention. Maureen never stops talking. I guess she's the opposite of me. Look at her! Even now during the rosary. Her hair's still a little messed up from the schoolyard. It's lighter brown than I remember and a little longer and thicker. She's more tan than the others but not as dark as Bernadette. She's not Italian. She's got freckles on her face and on her arms. Joey keeps squirmin' all around in his seat. He's got his feet spread way apart and his right leg's shakin' like mad. He can't sit still for the life of him. Keeps his hands folded, though. Colleen Hughes is built. Her back goes up in a big V like it was made especially to hold them up. Big shoulders. A shame she's not real pretty. She should donate what she has to Bernadette Falcone or Megan King. Wonder if she knows she stepped on that piece of gum. Did she do it today? Don't know. It's pretty dirty. Maureen's stacked, too — but hers aren't huge like Colleen's. They're just the right size for her body. She was one of the first ones to get them — one of the first ones I noticed, anyway. Yeah, they fit her body just right. Strong shoulders, too. That gum is driving me nuts. Maybe if she'd put her feet flat on the floor I could stop looking at it. Ed definitely sounds like he's asleep. What a bum! Joey sees him now. He's trying not to laugh. He'll wake him up before sister notices. Maybe! Look at that long hair on Megan King. It's so long and shiny — all the way down to the small of her back — and so blonde compared to Maureen's or Bernadette's. She's got a face like a statue's or a model's. Can't imagine liking her, though. She's almost too perfect. Never see her talking in class.

Number five. Halfway. Concentrate. Joyful mysteries. Annunciation. She knelt and the Angel Gabriel came and told her she was gonna have a baby. She was still frightened and extremely confused. She wasn't married after all. But she believed. She accepted. And the power of the Holy Spirit overshadowed her.

A stiff breeze shook the dogwood tree and tossed handfuls of petals into the air, leaving them to flutter in the window for a moment as they fell. In the top right hand corner of the blackboard, in a girl's handwriting — probably Megan King's handwriting — there was a reminder about returning May Procession forms.

The May Procession was coming up. The boys in blue blazers and girls in white dresses, everyone from First grade to Eighth grade, would assemble in perfect lines in the back of the school. They would march one head behind the other. When the cameras would flash from the buzzing crowds of parents and relatives, the children would not be able to turn their heads to see who was taking pictures. They would have to sing songs like "Immaculate Mary."

In Heaven, the blessed
Your glory proclaim.
On Earth, we, your children,
Invoke your sweet name.

The procession would go through the schoolyard while the sun burnt orange like charcoal and the smell of incense would come and go with the whims of the breezes.

The May Queen would be up front with Father Harrigan and she would place a crown of flowers on the head of the statue of Mary. Terrance took a deep breath and let it out slowly and silently. It was nice to think of the lines and lines of kids and the twilight and the flowers and the incense and the music. It relaxed him.

That Maureen never stops whispering and she's always got such mischief in her voice like she's got a secret. It's like she's done something wrong but it was worth it because it was fun. Her eyes are the same way. Light brown and with that mischievous glimmer. Like she's up to something. That voice! Fairly deep for a girl's and with that laugh in it. What the hell is she talking about, anyway? It's a wonder Sister lets those two sit together. You know her and Diane are gonna talk as long as they're together. It's a wonder she doesn't get herself into trouble more often than she does. The Nuns think she's a good girl: nice handwriting and good grades. So gullible! She does just enough. Rob's chewing on his pen as usual. He's up to his usual tricks. Doesn't know about Ed. Jim does. He's biting his nails. He can't look at Joey or he'll burst out laughing like he's gonna cough. It is pretty funny. Jim has a hard time keeping from cracking up. She's like that, too, but all the time. She always seems like her eyes are laughing and she can't keep from screaming for another minute, like she can't sit still, like she can't control herself. Those two better not start all that whispering and giggling during Math class. They get me all nervous and I miss some of the material. Maybe I'll have a different seat in that class, too. I don't need to be distracted sitting next to I DO and I DON'T. Maybe I'll ask her to change my seat, if she hasn't. What a couple of magpies! Heckle and Jekyll. One thing's for sure. I'm not gonna get a bad Math grade on my report for fooling around with them! But she's alright. She does get good grades. She was Student of the Month last year. That's how I got to know her name. She wasn't in my class then. She is crazy, though. A tramp, Mom would probly say. But I don't think so. Just a devil.

Was that number eight or number nine?

A giddiness came over Terry and he almost laughed out loud. His stomach muscles and then the rest of his muscles let go of their tension. For a moment, he wished he had his camera. He wanted to record the gum on the shoes, the silver crucifix, the nail biting, the golden hair of Megan King, the laughing eyes of Maureen Meehan, all the girls in all their varying stages of blossoming and development, the pen in Rob's mouth, the bowing heads, the sleepy postures, and the strange contortions of Joey. Then he decided he didn't need the camera. It was kind of fun without it. He had his eyes and his mind. He could watch these people, the same people from whom he had longed for praise this morning and over whom had wanted command, and he could record all of the things that they revealed to him, all of the things that they didn't even know about themselves.

It was number ten.

— ... as it was in the beginning,
   is now, and ever shall be ...

It's too bad Sister didn't pick somebody else to carry my books but it's nice of Michael Blaine to do it. It's easier to change classes from this seat in the back, also. Watching the rest of these people with all of their crazy habits and ways of doing things is — I don't know — amusing. They don't make me nervous. They're not a challenge at all.

— Before we begin class, Sister said, I'd like to welcome Terrance back to school after his long absence and remind him that he has been remembered in our prayers. We hope that his recovery is a complete and speedy one.

Some of the boys and some of the girls turned around to look at him. Many of them smiled. A few even clapped. Terrance smiled back and, despite the fact that he had dreamed of astounding everyone with his wit at this moment, answered with only a perfunctory:

— Thank you, Sister.

Sister instructed the students to take out their Religion textbooks and the children scrambled to do as they were told. Terrance was relieved at having been spared from embarrassment. The classroom grew quiet. Somehow it seemed that the cane beside him now marked him as wiser than he had been before.

The Bronx, Staten Island, Manhattan.
Completed March 1991.

Tulip Street

An occasional carhorn sent a fading note of complaint down the narrow brick walls of Tulip Street. Potholes made the car chassis grunt. A boy shouted. Some big dog's deep bark seemed to shake the whole block. In her little house, Danielle had gotten used to hearing and yet ignoring it all. She heard her mother's familiar step, tread, and creak downstairs. With her eyes closed, she could see her mother rushing around the kitchen. Toastsmell roamed into her room. Morning. It had long been morning. Daddy was going away. Back to the Navy. Her nightmare! Maybe this time he would not come back. No, she couldn't think that. It would never, ever come true. He promised.

Mom clanged utensils against pans and bowls and plates, whisking the eggs, putting a plate of stacked toast upon the table. She had called Danielle more than once, without success. Danielle was not sleeping or sleepy, but she did not want to move. She wanted to stay put, like a plant rooted in hard earth, and forget about her bad dream.

A man's voice in the kitchen, still strange though Daddy had been back from the Navy for a couple of weeks. She wondered what noises he hears, yet ignores when he is in his bunk at sea and if it is hard to learn to ignore them. The sea noises must be strange: the splashing against the steel walls, the hum of the engine, the cawing seagulls, the scratchy-snoring sailors. It must be weird to sleep below deck, knowing there is the ocean right outside and fish swimming alongside your room. She wondered if the fish could hear the snoring and if they ignored it.

— Danielle! I must have called you a half a dozen times now!

At breakfast, she wanted to ask him about sleeping on the boat. She kept thinking about the splashing, the humming, the cawing, and the snoring, and, about the fish swimming alongside his bedroom. But, she didn't dare ask. He seemed grouchy. He devoured his eggs and bacon with loudsmacking lips accompanied by snorting nostrils. He took big crunching bites of his toast, which seemed to follow a regular rhythm with his swallowing and his sips of orange juice. He sat up straight in his chair. He had sat that way when he had first gotten leave. He usually kept up the posture for a few days and then seemed to relax. Then he would seem happy to be home. It was as if everything were brand new to him. Or, maybe everything just seemed new and, at the same time, vaguely remembered, like a scene from another life or from a dream he had almost forgotten. Does it take him time to get used to the sea noises after he has been on land and to the land noises after he has been at sea? She wouldn't dare ask that either.

Now he had reached the restless stage, however, and his posture started to look like a sailor's again.

— I feel like a fish out of water around here! he had said last night.

Everything was suddenly kept in the wrong place. Everyone slept too much. Mom did not follow his instructions. And, life could not move fast enough. It was clear that he longed for the new life shipping out would bring — new but vaguely remembered, like a scene from another life or from a dream he had almost forgotten. But not that dream. Not her dream! Did he get tired of that life also after a while? Danielle thought so. But now she could see that he burned to be back eating breakfast among the men, with the floor under his feet rolling with the ocean waves.

— Did you sleep well, Danielle? he asked out of the blue.

— Pretty good.

His cold blue eyes squinted at her as he wiped his lips with a paper napkin.

— I thought I heard you yell somethin', he said. Did you have a nightmare?

The dream! The shock shook her to her bones. How did he know? What should she tell him? She felt so afraid for her daddy. Should she tell him about the dream? But then she was afraid of how he would react. He would think it was just silliness, probably. But, she had yelled something! What had she said? Did he already know what she had dreamed about? Had she given away some secret? She was dying to know.

— What did I say?

— I couldn't make out the words but you yelled out like you were in trouble or afraid of somethin'.

What could she say? She couldn't think up any story better than the truth.

— I had a dream about you, Daddy.

— Ha ha! he chuckled. About me, huh?

A storm! A storm! Her daddy on deck. The ship pitching wildly. Up and down. Left and right. Rough waves whitefoamed washing over the side, rising to his knees and ebbing away. Daddy's feet wet and cold. The wind screaming so loud it drowns his curses. He's moving away, moving away! Away! Mountains of seawater jump and plunge. The ship shrinks smaller and smaller! Lost! He'll be lost and gone! Daddy lost and gone!

— Yes, it was very scary. You were on a ship and there was a terrible storm. It was raining cats and dogs and the water was coming up onto the boat and making your feet wet and the wind was blowing and you were getting real mad.

It was strange that she always dreamed of a storm attacking him: never an enemy or a pirate ship or something. She guessed if any humans ever attacked her daddy in a dream, she could just imagine him shooting them and that would be the end of that.

— Ha ha! he laughed again. You had a dream about your old sailor daddy in a storm! Poor Danielle!

How could he laugh, she wondered. He didn't seem to understand the dream.

— But it was scary, Daddy. I didn't like the dream at all.

— Ah, it's nuthin' for a sailor to get his feet wet and curse at the wind.

He sniggered and snorted.

— But you were in trouble, Daddy.

— Danielle, you know I love bein' here with you and your mom. But ... But, there's another part of me that thinks my feet have been dry for too long now. Yih know what I mean?

He shuffled his feet underneath the table as if to illustrate his point.

— I have to go back to fightin' storms and cursin' at the wind. It's my way of life.

— I wish it wasn't. Danielle stomped her right foot. She stared into her plate of eggs for a moment, pouting. It's too scary with all the storms and big waves.

— Danielle! Her mother shouted. That's your father you're talking to!

— Also, I promised to serve in the Navy, her father added. I have to keep my promises — right? There's only another year to go. Plus, it's my duty.

— I always hated that word!

Her father chuckled and shuffled his legs about restlessly under the kitchen table. She couldn't believe it! All he could think about was getting back to sea, even in bad weather, and he didn't care about what the dream might mean.

As she left the house, she knew her mother was right. He had to pack his things and get ready for shipping out. It was his way. He had explained it many times.

— I don't know, he would say. I'm restless. I just can't stay on land all the time. Just be patient and I'll be back. I will always come back, Danielle.

The sea and the land, the sea and the land. Why did they have to be so separate? Why did one have to be different from the other? It was that way in the Bible. God parted the land from the sea. She wished He hadn't. But she shouldn't say that. Why couldn't Daddy love the land? Maybe there was some place where God hadn't parted the sea from the land, like an undersea island, like Atlantis. She wished she could go there. Maybe that could be her family's happy home. Or maybe she could wait there for him, at least, and each time he shipped out, she could watch the hull pass over her and see it go by again when he returned. Then she would know that it was almost time to see him. She could have a garden there and Daddy would love it because it would be land in the sea. But, maybe she could help him love the land more than the sea.

Since the springtime, Danielle's neighbor, Lena, had been letting her help in her patch of the community garden. She took care of the flowers and planted seeds. She learned how often to water this plant and how often to water that one. She memorized the names: the gladiolas and the tulips and the chrysanthemums and the irises and the orchids and the daisies. Lena had learned them from library books: city people didn't know much about these things, she said. Some names were hard to pronounce and her mouth and tongue were clumsy like a sailor without his sea legs. But the petals were so pretty and the feel of them in her finger tips made her feel so happy, she didn't care about the hard words. And, when the flowers were healthy looking and they were drinking up the water she had given them, she could have sworn they smiled at her. She remembered when she was little how she used to wonder how the plants could drink if they didn't have mouths. Then she learned about roots and saw how God gives them everything they need, even sending people like her and Lena to take care of them when they needed a little extra help.

Danielle had also helped harvest some of the vegetables, picking the tomatoes and some ears of corn. The way the bean stalks climbed up the poles was like magic.

They twisted like snakes — only nice snakes with no scary tongues or teeth! And the potatoes were so cute in their hiding spots underneath the broad green leaves and their little hills of dirt. Then there were the herbs which were like peppermint candy only not in a package but right there at your fingertips, little natural treats from God —and all you had to do was take care of them. And taking care of them made her so happy! She wished she were a farmer girl picking fruit and vegetables on a farm — like out in Lancaster where everything was spread out so wide and it seemed like you could look for miles over the fields to the horizon, as if the fields were an ocean of green, like down the shore, like Daddy's sea. But instead, she was on a small patch of dirt at Tulip and Cumberland surrounded by rowhouses on a hazy afternoon in noisy Port Richmond.

When he had first come home for leave, she had been so excited to tell her father about the plants she had learned about and taken care of so well that he had said:

— You better be careful or you'll turn into a plant!

But it was hard to stop talking about the garden. She wanted to share this newly discovered world with him. Her mother was pleased about it also, though she was critical of the dirt she dragged home on her clothes. Mom had even said that some of the tomatoes Lena had given her last week were better than Jersey tomatoes!

Lena noticed the effect the garden had had on Danielle.

— Danielle, she said. You love the garden — don't you?

— Yeah, I do.

— I can tell! You've been doin' a real good job with the flowers and all of the plants.

— Thanks, Lena.

— Well, I'll tell you what, Lena said with a broad smile. Next planting season, just before spring really starts, I'm going to save you a little patch of dirt right here.

She drew a little square in the air to trace the area of land which would be reserved.

— And I'm going to save it just for you. You can plant some of my seeds there and take care of it and it will be your very own section of the garden.

Her very own section of the garden! Could it be true?! She would take care of it as if it were her baby!

— And, Lena, can I still work on the rest of the garden, too?

Lena patted her protégé on the head.

— You can do as much as you like, sweetheart, as often as your mom let's you come.

— Lena, thank you so much!

She was so happy with this news that she barely noticed the thunder in the distance as she walked home. While they were having dinner, strong winds began to blow. Then, finally, the rain came. The drops seemed to attack the hot street. The people covered their heads and ran for home or whatever cover they could find. On Action News, they called it a Noreaster. Was it something to do with the Great Northeast? She didn't know. Anyway, it was something serious. Maybe it would keep her daddy home! God does give us everything we need!

Her bedroom window was left open just a little for some air and she could feel droplets of water blown through the screen. They kissed her feet with lips cold as death. The curtains of her window billowed like the sails of a ship from the olden days. She wondered if her daddy would like to sail in one of them. The stuffed animals and dolls in her room just stared in their usual, empty way, not smart enough to worry about anyone.

He can't go!

Whenever she closed her eyes: a storm! A storm! Her daddy on deck. The ship pitching wildly. Up and down. Left and right. Rough waves whitefoamed washing over the side, rising to his knees and ebbing away. Daddy's feet wet and cold. The wind screaming so loud it drowns his curses. He's moving away, moving away! Away! Mountains of seawater jump and plunge. The ship shrinks smaller and smaller! Lost! He'll be lost and gone! Daddy lost and gone!

He can't go!

The Noreaster was a being, an angry giant cloud with wicked blowing lips, blasting, screaming, and roaring. It bombarded the rooftops with hard, wetcold pellets, like countless boys throwing rocks.

Eventually, Danielle fell asleep, though she woke up shivering a couple of times. One time she thought she was on a ship at sea and that her room was tossing and turning. Another time, she had been dreaming that she was a woman about to get married on the grand island of Atlantis and before her wedding the stormy waters washed over the island and took her world away from her. Everything was water and destruction and death.

But, the sun was shining when she woke up and all she could hear were the usual street sounds.

When she came down for breakfast, she saw her father's bags in the living room. And he was in his uniform.

— But you can't leave, daddy! she shouted, tears starting to blur her vision of him. What about my dream? What about the storm? It was a Noreaster!

— Oh, sailors are used to storms, sweetie, he chuckled.

— Why are you always laughing? Danielle screamed.

She stomped toward the front door. As she reached it, she turned and shrieked:

— It's *not funny*!

She was racing down the street before she knew what she was doing. Her father walked after her, letting her run ahead. She needed to get it out of her system. Besides, he knew exactly where she was going.

When Danielle reached the garden, she stopped dead, panting and wheezing. The vegetables were all right but the *flowers* ... ! The Noreaster had chewed the flower garden to pieces. What had been a patch of earth smiling with color was now a swamp, a wasteland of mud. The flowers were all knocked down and drowned. They weren't even rooted in the earth anymore. The monster had ravaged her precious plantbabies. Tears came to her eyes before she could even catch her breath. She sat right down on the ground, not even caring about the mud.

An old black lady came over to her. She had seen the lady at the garden before but had never met her.

— What is it, sweetheart? The lady asked. Oh, honey, all your pretty flowers washed away!

She patted her on the hand but Danielle did not respond. Even though it was all muddy, Danielle covered her eyes with her other hand, and wept. Sadness rained down on her harder than the Noreaster had on Lena's little garden patch. Her tears dropped into the soft earth.

The lady crouched down next to her without getting dirty and shook her head at the little girl's lost garden of flowers.

— Nothin' I can say, sweetheart, the lady said. Except it's God's will. He give and He take away. The storm gave water to lots of plants that needed it but it destroyed this little patch of flowers. Nature do sloppy work sometime.

She laughed, hoping to get a smile out of the girl who was now sobbing quietly.

— Come on, honey, the lady said. It ain't so bad. You can grow a lot more pretty flowers. Who knows? Maybe one left even now.

Her eyes carefully explored the wreckage of the garden. Beyond a tiny hill of mud, she saw a dirtied splash of yellow and a healthy green stem rooted in the earth. The flower was bent over with its petals in the mud but it was still alive and healthy.

— Look! Look! she exclaimed. A iris! A pretty yellow iris — still alive!

— Danielle!

It was her father's voice from far away.

— Danielle!

He was walking across the street to her garden.

She looked back to the garden and saw where the lady was pointing. There was indeed a beautiful yellow iris, bent over and muddied, but still alive!

— Oh, thank you! Danielle cried.

Her father came up behind her. Danielle bent and plucked the flower out of the earth. Then, smiling through her tears, she handed to her daddy the muddied yellow iris, the survivor of storms.

Manhattan 2004.

Finding the Day

The Artist stepped off of the bus firmly resolved that he was better than any person with whom he had come in contact. Certainly none of his fellow students was equal with him.

Sie haben keine Phantasie! They are machines who do nothing but obtain information and give it back. They are merely computers, but, they are computers with a weakness — worry. They lack confidence in their own minds' abilities to think. They simply swallow the words of their teachers and belch them back onto mimeograph paper. No thinking. No reflection. No imagination.

— Yo!

The Artist, moving south on Seventeenth Street, was about to cross John F. Kennedy Boulevard when he recognized the voice, and, with some hesitation, turned around to see his younger friend and schoolmate.

— Hey, Will.

Will motioned for The Artist to come along with him to the El. All through his Greek, History, Latin, Religion, English, Math, and German classes, the sixteen-year-old Artist had suffered the company of his fellow students. Now the day was over.

No way. Not today. I'm not going with him just because he sees me and needs someone to hold his hand!

— Whatsa matter with your brother?

— What do you mean?

— I saw him today and he was going off somewhere by himself instead of taking the El home.

Then he'll condemn me by bopping the side of his head with his index finger. He can talk about me behind my back, if he wants to. He can think what he likes. I don't care about these people any more. I'm on a higher plane. They don't understand.

The Artist hastened away without another word. Knowing that the light was about to change, he started across JFK before the traffic had come to a complete halt. He took note of the businessmen and the secretaries who hesitated on the corner. Their cowardice corroborated his assumption of superiority.

"GO PHILLIES! GO PHILLIES!" shout the October business windows. Toy helicopter with propellers twirling on a vendor's stand. An elephant beating a drum next to it. The beat fades and vanishes. A good one! The beating of youth's drum fading and vanishing as I become a man. Cymbal. Nice pair of tits.

The Artist reached Chestnut Street and went left.

A Greek restaurant. We should all go there on a class trip. Crackle of the P.A.: "All students interested in going to the Greek restaurant will leave after sixth period today."

Stopping, The Artist scanned the blue letters on the white sign for words from ancient Greek. His tired eyes began to sting. He found no familiar words. His throat was dry.

No. This is modern Greece. Nothing to do with what we're studying. It's too hot out for this coat. I'm tired — in body and in spirit.

He left the sign. Music rose from a violin. Half a block away, a blonde-haired man wearing a blue-flannel shirt bowed his instrument with great confidence and with great indifference to the crowd that was gathering around him. Moving closer, The Artist noticed a black man with the violinist. He was playing a guitar and singing. He wore a long beige coat and a white hat with a black band. The front of its rim was turned up. The violinist wore jeans and leather boots. The pitch and volume of the violin soared over the deep, regular strumming of the guitar. The Artist crossed Chestnut, dropped his heavy bag upon the sidewalk, and joined the audience.

He felt his soul rise with the music and seem to fly away from his dirty, busy environment. None of the bored frustration, of the fatigue, or of the emotional torment afflicting him was proof against it. For a few moments, the burning ache of violent contempt for all and for everything was soothed by the straining violin and the rhythmic guitar. He whirled around with his hands thrust deep in his pants pockets and peered down the street. On both sides in well-ordered lines among the scraggly trees trying on their autumn attire flew Star-Spangled Banners. New red-white-and-blue SEPTA buses paused and opened their doors for waiting commuters. Cars, vans, taxis, and a motorcycle travelled sporadically south on Fifteenth. Two cops in black leather and shiny silver badges chatted with a young secretary in front of Zounds and another, looking bored, strolled toward the crowd in which The Artist stood. Pedestrians crossed the street over the imitation cobblestone walkway. Orange "DON'T WALK" signs blinked and yellow caution lights flashed. He turned again toward the musicians.

In the weak yellow spotlight falling at a narrow angle from the tired sun, the guitar player sang with feeling. He nodded and shook and swung his head and generously lit up his very white smile.

They like him. He'd make a good politician. I don't have any money — just tokens. Wait. Here's a dime.

— *Sm ... i ... i ... i ... i ... le!*

Oh! Another good one. The beauty of it all. The flag-lined streets and the people flitting here and there! Abandon is here. Good. It is pleasure.

A little boy approached the guitar case that lay in front of the musicians. He swung his clenched fist over the case a few times, as if he needed to warm up, and then let the change his mother had given him fall from his hand.

I can't. Its only a dime. It's better than nothing. No, it isn't. If I put in a dime, I will get a sneer but if I don't and slip away unseen, nothing unpleasant happens.

The Artist picked up his schoolbag and walked away in wordless thought. A blind man shook his cup and tapped his cane in the middle of the sidewalk. The Artist with only a dime to spare passed by with the rest of the pedestrians.

Pinball! Man-boys playing spaceman in their businessman suits. Their attaché cases are next to the machines. I am their opposite. I am a boyman. I am a boy becoming a man. Nice-looking girls smoking on a bench. Wo! An apeman!

The man in the ape suit stepped toward him. He placed a paw on The Artist's back and pointed with the other one toward Spencer's Gifts. In the window, there was a life-sized poster of Cheryl Ladd wearing a pink, low-cut top and short cut-off jeans. It was surrounded by toys.

Get away. Run! Why? It can't hurt. Just move a bit closer.

The smoke curling up in their faces, the girls cried:

— Awlright! Awlright!

The impatient apeman shook his hairy finger at the door.

— Ah, ... no, thanks.

— Awww! Boooooooo!

There's no way he's going to make a fool of me — especially in front of these girls. *Go to hell*!

He got a safe distance away from his tormentors and then slowed down. He wasn't interested in them or in that stuff. His soul was wrestling with Love. The burdens yoked to his body and soul, he knew, had been quarried by unreturned Love — Love unreturned to him and Love which he failed to return. The boyman shuffled to the corner of Fifteenth and Chestnut.

A man of doubtful heterosexuality leaned limply against the wall. The Artist crossed to the other side of the street.

Woman in a man's body. Man who loves men. Unnatural but love. Love is the point. Love is the burden and the meaning. Stupid students miss the point. They rebel against their future selves. They scream like uncomfortable babies who want their diapers changed. They never get beyond that. Their rage is temporary, a "phase." It wants a change of externals. To love and be loved is it. *Nicht Geld*! "To love and be loved by me."

There's the lawyer. He's no fool.

Doesn't know the Golden Rule.
There's the Doctor, yes, indeed.
Has forgot the Apostles' Creed.

All professions great and small
Lead many a man to fall, to fall
Into the depths of old routine
But in the end life's not so clean.

Not real clean? Becomes unclean? Een een een. Now? No. When we get home. *Tips for Stage Productions.*

The book in the window of B. Dalton Bookseller halted him. To his disgust, The Artist found that the book was intended for stage hands and managers — not for writers.

Of course not.

The Artist proceeded toward the revolving door.

A haunt of Freshman days it is. A visit will revive me, will be a rest from the cruel night of suffering whose shadows my gift has gathered and whose opaque blackness my Love has painted.

Medea wailing violence, shrieking blood-red hate. Black-hearted hate remorseless and bitter. Her love now hate. Weakness. I am better. I still love. School again. Wasting my time? Possibly. A skeleton in the window. I didn't even notice it! I must be on a different plane! Higher or lower? Better or worse? Higher and better. My reflection in the window. My grey cap, my suit coat, tie, shirt … my belt and pants. Bag of books in my hand. My pale face shocked next to the skeleton's. I wonder if it's real. Seems more real than me. Was probably the playwright. His face is stiff, bony, hard. Mine is airy, an illusion of light. A reflection. Like a ghost. Spirit. Spiritual reflection. Father Tuar in class today said it's good. I reflect but they don't. But every day? Does that make you better? Oh, I don't know. I don't know.

Waves of thought pound endlessly on the shores of the mind! Some are small and repetitive. Others are somehow dangerous.

The Artist entered the bookstore.

The Ewings of Dallas.

He chuckled.

I'm breaking through a barrier of strange eyes that see only a boy. They don't want me here.

— What's he doing here? Kid must be a weirdo.

— What's a young kid like that doing in a bookstore on a day like today?

— Wandering around here by himself on such a beautiful afternoon?! There's definitely something wrong with this kid.

ART

He approached the shelf and dropped his schoolbag on the floor. His mind began to fashion a chain from his flashing, jumbled thoughts. He delighted in the beginning of clarity and order.

Remember the waves and the haunt of Freshman days and the opaque blackness my Love has painted and the musicians in the street, trying to make a living. All professions great and small lead many a man to fall, to fall. The apeman with the toys and the girls with the smoke in their eyes. And how about ... ?

The burden on his spirit now lightened.

Creative Water Color Painting.

Perfect! Art means painting to the modern man. Certainly the authors know and the owners of the store must know but, of course, they are expected to cater to those who think of it as "arts and crafts class." The waves are growing and becoming gentler. I feel something stirring deep in the caverns of my mind. I understand and so am better.

He flipped through a weighty art-history book. Ancient, grey, stone faces stared at him from Celtic crosses. He read:

"Medieval Irish art often expressed the idea of the individual attached to a society. Man is one; he is one of many."

If you are better, why don't you prove it? Reflection is good but what are its results?

Remember the *Tips for Stage Productions* and *Creative Water Color Painting*, the modern Greeks, the fading drumbeat of youth, leaving Will at the bus stop. When we get home. When we get home.

The Artist replaced the book and wandered from the Art section, preoccupied with the growing gentleness of the waves. He grabbed a large picture book from a nearby bin, without looking at its cover. He opened it and was surprised to see Bo Derek kneeling on a beach with a wet white blouse clinging to the contours of her body. With quiet disgust, he tossed the embarrassment on top of a pile and fled. Hot shame expanded under his cheeks.

Everyone is looking at me now. All men have eyes. Lurking behind them is the mind forming ideas and impressions, making judgments, casting away the rejects and the queers and welcoming the nice, normal ones. The waves grow rough and quick. They erode my good mood. Pedestrians passing in the big window.

STRUM, STRUM, STRUM, STRUM.

Can't forget the businessmen hesitating at the light, or playing spaceman, or the gay man, or the apeman, or the blind man, or the boyman. What about me?

The Artist worried about himself. He wondered how long he could keep up his insular existence. He sensed that it was dangerous to his health, that retreating from the scattered urban herd was good but that it could be done excessively. Retreating, even if onto a pedestal, should not be done too often.

Parens, Adolescens, Adultus.

Three circles on the board. Together? Adulthood. Separate? Childhood? Retreating into the circle of thought, which teenagers often do, can cause mental illness. That's what Mr. Apprendi had said in Greek class.

Anxiety overcame him for a moment. He trusted Mr. Apprendi. The Artist knew that when the teacher went off on a tangent like that, spinning images with his words and seeming to shape them with his hands into an object to look upon with respect and awe, that he only consented to do so because he had some valuable lesson to impart.

He was right. I've been fighting off the enclosing world with my words. My words are daggers flung from my mouth. Their release is pleasure. What are the results, though? Sharp points burrowing into the hearts of those in my inner circle. They retaliate with daggers of their own.

Everyone's waves grow swift and eroding. She did the same to me but does not know it.

POETRY

The Artist chose a book by Patrick Kavanaugh. He examined the green cover, turning the volume over and sliding his right hand into his pants' pocket.

— Look at this kid reading a poetry book!

— What's he doin' in here?

— He's got a bag with him. Watch him!

God! I wish these people would leave me alone! So what? I can read a poetry book if I want to.

"Patrick Kavanaugh is known for his writing about Irish poverty."

The Artist unconsciously toyed with the dime in his pocket.

In class, he said that you can reflect by reading poetry. Reflection. Reflection is good. But shouldn't it be followed by actions?

An older man passed by The Artist. He slapped the book shut.

— *Vestehen Sie Deutsch? Bücher zu!*

Sue! She'll like a poet — won't she? I don't know. Who cares?

He couldn't let the stomach pang associated with her name nor the blonde, blue-eyed image that it always conjured up to take control of him. If allowed to evolve from a sound to an image to a feeling, the name never failed to hurl him and whatever he had of peace or pleasure howling down the dark, winding abyss of despair.

Afterwards, the smile that had been on his face would always seem revolting, the moment of peace he had had would seem only to have whetted his soul for more torture, and the sunshine would seem a mockery, a popular, deceitful truism. However, this time his intellect promptly halted her name. It would proceed no further. Smooth and placid would be the ebb and flow of the waves.

James Kavanaugh. Oh, he's American. So am I. *Celebrate the Sun*. How can I if I can't even see it? T.S. Eliot. I've heard of him.

A woman stopped to look at the same shelf of books which held The Artist's attention. The Artist turned his back on her and walked to the other side of the case. He felt the familiar forming of images. The thing was indeed coming to life in a deep, unexplored cavern of his mind. Perhaps its birth would cause the sun to burst again through the grey, swirling clouds.

The strumming of the guitar and the soaring of the violin notes. Remember that. Remember the flags on Chestnut Street and the yellow lights. Remember the burdens, the heavy bag and the suit coat. From? The bus stop. Not now. Soon.

William Butler Yeats. I know that name, too. Yeah: "I will arise and go now, and go to Innisfree."

Another customer, a businessman, interrupted The Artist. He was distracted from Yeats. His eyes fell on another book: *Best Loved Modern Poetry*.

Yeah, like:

There once was a man from Peru
Who took a trip on a canoe.
While dreaming of Venus,
He played with his penis
And wound up with a handful of goo.

Oh, yes! Oh, yes! It must be included. The raging Artist poking fun at the tastes of modern America! But, what about- Oh, so what?

The image, newly born, had escaped the cavern and begun its ascent, despite the sheerest cliffs and sharpest rocks. The Artist laughed to himself and for a brief moment his soul exulted in its superiority.

But if you are better, why don't you prove it? How? How? How? Back to Yeats.

A blind man walked by the window, tapping his cane.

How? How? How?

Back to Yeats, damn it! No. Wait a minute. Love is the meaning of life — remember that? You must give in order to love. Love means action. But I am on a higher plane than these people. No, it's a different plane and one which exists for the service of theirs. How can you be on the plane you say you are on and see the drudgery of everyday life and not attempt to use your creative abilities to help them?

He played with the dime in his pocket again. The Artist hid his eyes in the volume of poetry. He read "To A Young Beauty":

Dear fellow-artist, why so free
With every sort of company
With every Jack and Jill?
Choose your companions from the best;
Who draws his bucket with the rest
Soon topples down the hill.

If he had read those lines a few moments earlier, if he had cast his eyes upon the poem without having first seen the blind man go by, then its sentiment would have cemented his feeling of superiority. The old master's theme would have convinced him of his own existence on a higher plane. However, he had seen the blind man go by and now the poem's music was in the wrong key; its melody was disturbing. He was not necessarily better but different — maybe. Certainty fled faster than reason.

The creative level of existence is obviously better than the one that seeks entertainment! The changing waves! The caves with the creature climbing from the depths to be born! I am better than someone who just interprets other people's works! The audience, the actors are not as good as writers!

Having replaced the Yeats volume, he started walking out of the store.

Will it be good?

He was passing the Art section when, still unable to face his fellow creatures, he lowered his eyes and side-stepped a businessman.

Cezanne

— Suzanne's not here. She went down the shore.

His intellect slammed shut a thick, steel, cold door.

How? How? How?

Prove yourself! You are on a higher, different, or whatever kind of plane and yet you show no results of being on that plane. The long night is still here. If your reflection is followed by an act, it may come to an end. To love and be loved but also to do!

He entered the world, heard its beeping cars, saw and felt its people rushing in the twilight. He shuffled, still in the grip of his thoughtworld, around the corner.

Εισ ανερ ουδεισ ανερ. This insular existence is wrong. Reflection is important but it cannot become a complete retreat. You are part of the world whether you like it or not.

The Artist sighed at the cars jammed up at the intersection.

Celebrate the Sun?! Where is it?

Over the din of carhorns beeping, a radio blared:

— Though the night's so long, boy, you can find the day!

There was no more violin music in the street but its beauty in contrast with the strumming guitar remained, resounding in his ears.

A blind man passed.

Even if it's only a dime, it's what you have and should be given to the blind.

He put the dime into the blind man's cup.

Drafted Philadelphia October 1980.
Revised Staten Island, Manhattan 1991, 2002.

It's All Abandoned

Lily turned the other knob and reached for a towel. Outside, a gentle, slow, and unspectacular sunset marked with receding light the sun's retreat from the South Bronx sky. She could see a dull sliver of it through the dirty window. Even though the window was closed, the twilight air could still sneak in. No man in the house long enough to fix things and that stupid super never did nothing. The cold air raised gooseflesh on the brown skin of her skinny adolescent body and she muttered her little Spanish rhyme:

— *¡Frio! ¡Frio! ¡Dios mio!*

A plane from LaGuardia shook the decrepit tenement. Kitchen sounds came from the other side of the door. As Lily dried herself, she imagined her mother washing the noisy dishes. She listened to the insistent rush of water into the soapy dirty pool in the basin of the sink. She heard silverware being sorted by her older sister, Cassandra, the crash of utensil upon utensil as each knife, fork, and spoon dropped into its proper place. And the little T.V. shouted deep-voiced advertisements in Spanish. With the towel wrapped around her modest body, she rushed through the kitchen.

Rosa, her baby sister, charged into the kitchen with a lollipop in her mouth.

— *¡Ay, Dio'! ¡Sucia!*

Her mother took the dishtowel and cleaned the baby's sticky mouth.

Lily skipped around her baby sister and bumped into the kitchen table. A Santeria candle fell down. Her mother yelled. But Lily kept on. She hated the cold air and the sight and sound of her mother. The hum of the blow drier drowned out the kitchen sounds when she was safely cocooned in her bedroom. What would she wear? Black. Black was the color for tonight. She pulled down the shade of her window and dropped the damp towel on the bed. Quickly, she chose a pair of panties from the drawer and stepped into them. Next was a black bra. She fastened it around her abdomen and quickly slipped her arms through the straps without looking at herself. Another plane roared over the roof. Bass notes thumped from a passing car. An ice cream truck played "Here Comes Mr. Softee" over and over. It was the sound of summer.

The water stopped flowing in the kitchen. She knew her mother was coming to the door, holding the towel still in her hand. She knew already what her words would be:

You ready?

Lily took her black dress from the closet and was examining it for wrinkles, spots, or lint, when the voice came from the other room.

— You ready?

— Not yet.

Hurry up!

— Hurry up!

She sighed and slumped down on the edge of her bed. She was not a dog to jump when her master yelled.

— *¡Stupida! ¡Loca!*

The doorbell dingdonged and the sound of her mother's heels went over to the door. It was Grandma, from her house downstairs.

— I'm going down to start up the car. If you're not ready in two minutes, I'm leaving. You're not the only one with plans tonight. ¡*Dese prisa 'hora mismo!*

— Oh, fuck you, she whispered.

She'd say it to her face someday. She knew she would. Let her leave without her and find something to fuck tonight. She wasn't scared to walk. She was armed. That was right. She couldn't forget that. The knife was in her other purse.

Downstairs that stupid dog was barking again.

— ¡*Quiet te!*

She stood up and hurriedly got into her dress. As her bare foot entered her high-heeled shoe, Lily realized that she had not put on her pantyhose. A stream of Spanish curses flowed from her. Her mother was forever doing that to her. She always nagged her about this and this and this and this and this and this and that 'til she made her so crazy she forgot what she was doing. If she would let her get ready without asking her "Are you ready?" she would get ready faster. You would think an old person would know that.

Anyway, she was going to have fun tonight, to shine in front of those bitches and those nerd teachers. Those teachers! She didn't need them and their detentions and their superior clauses and propositional phrases or whatever. She would look fly and dance with the cutest guy in the place. Those teachers really didn't know her. They didn't care either. She knew what's up. It was true that she was just fifteen but she knew a lot. Those Americans don't know what time it is. This is the South Bronx! And those girls! They had only seen her in her uniform from school. That was not her. They would see.

Lily made herself up in purple eyeshadow and thickly coated her lips in pink. Then she put on her coat and came into the kitchen.

Her squat, square-shaped Grandma was standing there holding Rosa. Lily kissed her Grandma.

— You cut your hair? Lily asked.

— No, no. I just changed the color.

— Looks *nice*!

It was a copper color like her best friend Cynthia's. And, she did like it.

Lily clopped down the steps to the street, making an ugly face at the cooking smells. As she reached the sidewalk, she started getting excited. Her mother complained and yelled at her, at the cars in front of her, about the time, about how long it had taken her daughter to get ready, and why had she worn that depressing black dress. It was the usual shit from her mother and she paid it no mind. She was just glad to be out of her house, to see the dark streets, the flashing lights of the bodegas, the passing cars with music playing, and the people who walked this way and that.

She danced to the rap music with a couple of the girls and then with her best friend, Cynthia. There seemed to be plenty of time. At about 11:30, some sleazy guy who thought he was Bobby Brown started dancing with her little whore friend. They left her to lean against the wall near where the teachers stood looking authoritarian and bored. The teachers checked their watches and screamed words into one another's ears as lights flashed and MCs rhymed and DJs scratched. Teenage shoulders jerked and teenage heads bopped both up and down and back and forth. It was a sea of shadows she saw, with no special identity, jerking, bouncing, breaking, in the rhythmically broken darkness. The dance maybe could be anywhere, Lily thought, but it wasn't. They were kids she knew in a place she knew and didn't, couldn't ever like. They were kids that no one liked in a place that wasn't liked and had been and would always be abandoned.

Minerva had said that word. She told the gym teacher, "I don't like playing in this field. It's all abandoned."

It was a good word. It fit. No one lived there. Rats and bums and stray dogs had taken over what real people had abandoned. The buildings had been arsoned and covered with tags by writers who were jailed or dead or made worthless by dope. Trash, bricks, broken glass, car parts, and dog shit covered the outfield. Kids used mattresses for trampolines, car hoods for sleds, and forever-drooling fire hydrants for refreshment. It was all abandoned. Lily awoke from her angry reverie and watched again the adolescent shadows move in eerie unison. She was bored.

At quarter to twelve, the DJs started giving slow songs. The dance was ending. Only clinging couples now populated the floor. Suddenly, Lily remembered that this was what she had come for. This was the moment when Romance was to walk up, take her by the hand, and dance with her to New Edition's "Earth Angel."

— I hope she catches AIDS, the girl muttered, watching Cynthia giving some tongue to that guy.

She hoped no one would ask her. The dance was almost over. What was the point? There wasn't a point. What was a point anyway? Something that stabs you or you stab someone with. She smiled. Good thing she was thinking and not talking or they'd come and lock her up in one of those homes like what happened to that girl last year who tried to kill herself.

One slow song ended and another began. Nothing changed. No one would ask her, she knew. It was too hot anyway and besides there were no cute guys. Even if there were, they were only interested in one thing. The DJ threw on "Earth Angel." Why did he have to play that one? She hoped somebody would ask her. Maybe someone would. Maybe Romance was just shy. What would she say to him when he made his move? She had nothing to say. She was boring. She worried over nothing. No one would ask her. She looked around at the dancing boys. Romance must have stayed at home tonight. Good.

The song was half over. Why hadn't anyone asked her? She had danced with Cynthia and the other girls but she felt like dancing with a guy. Maybe it was because she was a stick. Guys don't like sticks. It didn't matter. Who did she want to dance with anyway? No one. No one was worth the trouble — the butterflies going crazy in her stomach, the jokes from the girls on Monday. The lights came on. She, like her place, had been abandoned.

Her mother stood at the top of the stairs barking at her, early for once in her life. Lily grunted in answer to all her mother's questions. The woman seemed hurt. Maybe she was truly trying to be friendly and interested. But what did Lily have to say? Nothing. Nothing had happened. No one had asked her. There was nothing to say.

Cassandra buzzed Lily in.

— What happened?

— Nothing.

— Who did you dance with?

— No one.

— Oh, come on! she sang. You can tell meeeee!!

— I'm tired.

Lily plodded into her room and sat feeling stupid and wide-awake on the edge of the bed. Hadn't she been sitting here a few hours ago in this same place looking forward to her fun? Now it was over and she was not even sweaty. She was just as clean as when she'd gone out. She thought of the guy, Junior, across the street who came home from every baseball game in a bright clean uniform. Everyone knew he hadn't played. She was like him. Her hair was exactly the same as it had been when she'd sat here before. She had met no one. She had given her phone number to no one. No one would call. What had she to look forward to now? Nothing. Another Monday morning would chill her. More classes would bore her. She'd fail more tests and nothing would change and no one would call. It hurt so much remembering how she had looked forward to the dance and thinking how nothing had happened that without wanting to, she began to cry.

Tears smeared her mascara and trickled over the cheekbones she had tried to highlight like the magazine said to. Nothing to look forward to. Nothing to do. She decided to never look forward to anything again as long as she lived. It was foolish to get excited about the future.

The future ... As long as she lived ... How long would that be? Not long, she hoped. Maybe she would mess up and do crack and someone would pay attention to her. There was little chance of getting pregnant. Anyway, those guidance counselors and social worker nerds would be in her business. She didn't want that. Maybe she would do what that girl did last year and what those rich American kids did. She never understood why she had to carry so much pain around with her all the time everywhere. Maybe she would just put an end to all the pain. Besides, if she messed up, no one would come visit her in the hospital and nothing would be solved.

She tried to be as slick as possible going to the bathroom to get her lady shaver. Slitting her wrists would be good and bloody. Bright red blood oozing on her black dress. What would the magazines say about that? Black had been perfect for tonight. She was certain now.

Lily sat up in her bed and pushed back her sleeve. She examined the veins in her left forearm. She held the blade poised over her wrist for several seconds. A profound tiredness quickly overcame her. She placed the shaver down on her nightstand, and, as if drunk, fell into a deep slumber with all of her clothes on.

The sun would rise again at dawn and some light would come through the dirty window of her bedroom. Her mother would wake her and nag her all day as always. Cassandra would bother her all day with questions. School, as usual, would bore her. Her abandoned life would go on in the same way in this abandoned place because she had gotten tired and for the rest of her life she would never understand any of it nor ever figure out why she had done that.

Drafted The Bronx 1987.
Revised Manhattan 2002.

IYouHeSheIt

... And so we have the courage to say ...

Yeah! You were the one, yeah, yeah, you were the one I saw but I know you won't admit it. You were the one lying in the darkness, thinking, sighing, staring at a rainbowed streetlight.

... so much uncertainty of loneliness. Thin voices dreamy haunt on the screen of the wide mind in a twisting body wrestling with something, some unseen being, some creature, somewhere, somehow. *Ego, I, mich, me,* somewarehouse, sum of things, groans, and words. Defeat. Sleepy death wish. Screams, desires, strange positions. Repulsion. Reclusion. Recline.

Why didn't I ever notice the clouds before at night? You wanted to fly off of your bench away from the faces cast onto the moon and the lights.

Yours were the eyes that wandered alone the length of the white path that climbed lazily up the golfcourse's night-covered hill as the trees rained in dartlike twigs on your wondering mind.

Your cloudy brain's voice trembled as it screamed, "Death to Sadness!" at the sky. You didn't have to stumble backward very far, though, to find arguments or at least contradictions to you feeble war cry.

... In the name of the Father ...

The doors of your metal magic carpet had mercilessly hissed and pounded together, pounding the endless song into your head: Pain! Sigh! Pain! Sigh! Pain! Sigh! You had run to your bus, sweating under your heavy jacket on that icy-aired afternoon. Finding some daylight in the backseat, you rushed for it.

You let your pacified eyelids slide over your vision as you began thinking ... of nice things, as Dad used to tell you to do when you were battling a nightmare.

Uncle Jimmy's boat. Leprechauns on skateboards. Long-haired "hippies." Look at that! You can't tell whether that's a boy or a girl.

Threw a ball at the ceiling, while lying on the floor. Gonna be president, solve the dangerous drug abuse dilemma. Gonna solve the prejudice problem. People with pimples were drug addicts who put nasty things in your apples on Halloween.

Drug commercials were scary. Needless needles and pills chasing some boy. Music was weird in the background.

"I Want To Hold Your Hand!" Practicing with my little guitar and with go-go dancers from across the street. Tambourines. Lotsa noise.

St. Paddy's Day party. "Gilly Gilly" music only good on that day. The lights shone through the lights in their glasses ...

... and through the blue windows in the neat, clean, different-songed Protestant church with its little boxes for its hardback hymnals. Wanted to correct ladies about what they said about Moses but didn't bother. 'd be a brat.

Played in a box surrounded by mud with the bully down the block — astronauts and their rocketships. Countdown! Fire! Cool!

So were the battles on the news. We were undefeated in wars. Dad twisted my arm. Mom said he was cruel like the Vietcong. He thought it was funny. I got away and ran across the street — too sensitive.

Lady across the street was always working on her lawn. Didn't like our dog who usta jump up and look at everything from his closed up "second part," putting his front paws on the top of the bottom half of the separating door.

My cousin took his picture. She was from Connecticut. A lot of rocks. Antique yellow car. Tears at departure. Her face in the dark at the back of Steve's house even a year later.

The bus ripped you from your chosen spot in space with cruel, blue-cushioned claws.

... *And of the Son* ...

The song of the bus became the annoying pop of your radio alarm in the morning, which became an enemy you couldn't smack back, which always made you submit to consciousness. You opened your eyes to be wrapped up in a chrome bandana that crushed your head like a boa constrictor. Your ears were greeted by the groaning bus that seemed like the deafening souls of schoolmates and the voices of forgotten friends that echoed inside your hungry brain. You tried to skate across your breath to dim hollow caves of peace — to hide silently under layers of volume the way you used to hide under your blanket in your playpen. But, in this self-deceiving "obscurity," you could not die or go blind — you could still see the skeletons that supported the flesh that hid under the skin. You were being worn down like the pencils you had watched being sharpened today. Mommy's and Daddy's advice would not help you now as the situation continued to deteriorate.

— Remember when they were little?

— Good old days.

You now searched for substitute parents as your wrists thirsted for crucifixion. Despite the many with whom you could share the transcendentally silly glances of friendship, you felt that there was no one, no one, no one whom you could talk to. There was something inside of you, something so strange, and so mystical — like a pun that would sum up the questions and answers of the Universe — that you didn't dare to read it much less communicate it. Maybe you wouldn't understand it even if you did look at it. But it was there and you know it

You could feel it rumbling like the engine you sat next to, bumping over potholes, perpetually coughing, always burning, restless every moment. You wanted to drown it, at least for a few hours. You wished that somehow you could expel it. Your mind was fixed on it and escaping from it. There was nothing else. Nothing else in the world.

... And of the Holy Spirit ...

Even your dreams were haunted with sadness. It crept in under the boardwalk that you had been running along. Foaming lazily, it left its mark like a weary student dropping his books at the end of a week. Even though dolphins could fly and the icy stars illuminated your thoughts, the mournful tune was unstoppable. Like a romantic, cliché-filled, old song, it seeped through the cracks that you stood on. You wept.

You got out of your seat and walked up the aisle, looking out the window and listening to the seated people.

Rainy fall that sweats like the summa.

Personifications of weakness with strong voices forgot to open the blinds when they left the house.

The bus grudgingly hissed to a stop, spit you out, and passed away. Your heavy legs carried you home to eat dinner. You started to feel philosophical.

An unrestricted God who lovingly restricts his sons and daughters must hate his own existence. Urizen the Lawgiver must hate himself, must hate his very nature enough to prevent us from it. Seasons pass like every second without doors, bars, cables, walls, windows, locks, keys, or warnings.

Memories began to dial and ring calling you even further backward and into an even smaller box.

It looked like an angry piece of stormcloud fallen from the sky and hardened by its landing. To the right of it rested a graveyard; to the left of it some sore-thumb houses, which stuck out like artificial smiles on depressed faces. Some divine adhesive had cemented your lips together and your red eyes to that road.

Someone sings about wanting a slow hand. Someone else is still crazy after all these years and still another wonders if everything's all right.

Still no one ...

A light green terrycloth cover-up had followed a pair of long legs down that street. A pair of brown eyes that seemed able to soak up the entire world even while confused and angry.

No movement ...

The ladies were there, as usual, sitting by the pool. The snack bar lady was still fat, her daughter still spoiled.

The trees boxed, wrestled, or, perhaps, laughed with the wind. The water was still bouncing up and down, glistening with what was left of the sunlight. Wanted to take a giant fishing rod and reel in the sun. Just sittin' here tryin' to bury its brightness and fill in the ditches of time. Workin' hard just to finish buryin' each moment, wantin' another day to pass 'cause I know she ain't gonna be here.

Not even a leaf or a piece of paper moves on that street.

No energy. Fuzzy memory. Cars meander into alleys at dinnertime. Mouth-closed message:

Oh, angry beaten street, you are my hope. You, the angry past and future, have control of my eyes and my tongue. I no longer feel a part of this world but apart from it. The present is only a stepping stone to the future. The past is a T.V. show impossible to turn off. And the future lies somewhere on you, street ... or perhaps on the sidewalks ... or hiding in your cracks. The lash marks on your blue hide pain me so greatly. I know that somehow you are my future face. You shall be my home, death, rest. Why must you keep me hungry and so restless in my silent stillness? Why must you tease me with your magic hope dangling on an unreachable string? Why must you whip me the way you've been beaten?

Still empty ...

She ain't gonna be here..

She ain't gonna be here.

She ain't gonna be here.

The show that you were watching was really boring. (Or was it you?) The couch's cushions barely touched your numb back. It became again a bench on a golf course by a lake. Someone came smiling, slipping down the fairway, no part of her body in motion.

She came out of the past, a blonde shadow of the sun. Your boyhood was carried in her pigtails. She had grown older and beautiful without losing her childlike cuteness. You talked. The words came out soft and cool like a little creek that you used to throw stones into when the world was a lot sunnier and you thought little seeds could grow into huge trees and you could come back and carve your initials into them. You could pass by and tell your children and grandchildren, "I planted that tree. It was just a seed when I was a little kid and we planted it. Now look at it! Wow!" (You knew better than that now.)

You stared at her beauty and wondered was she as lonely as you. You told her of your unsuccessful search for love — about the green-terrycloth girl and the power of the snowy flesh that strode so beautifully and precisely under the fiery hair. Both of them had hammered the nails deeper through your wrists and into the wood you had rested on your entire life: thank God for Himself! He did it. Made it holy. Death, resurrection, and all that good stuff. You told her of the void you felt, of the hollow tree of life that stood at the core of every breath you took. (You thought that was extremely clever, mystic, and deep as all hell.)

No reaction ...

You told her how tired you were and that that was why you were lying there alone and why you were so happy she came along for someone for you to talk to, to let you empty out everything that had been building up inside you. You told her how sincere and revealing you were being. You called to her from across a transparent wall, telling her how desperate and supremely alone you were.

Was the door locked upstairs? No one's home. It's cool.

An approach. You knelt.

With all of your dreams and with all of their despair and weariness drooled out of you, you wrapped your arms tightly around her pulsing frame. The two of you curled up together like infants (or people even younger.) You couldn't see a thing but you could sense the soft peace in her breathing. Again, you wondered what she thought as you drifted like a tiny piece of wood down your own personal stream.

There is no true silence when it rains. No break in conversation. It drummed on the roof of the blue Nova on my first morning of kindergarten (with bigger drops.) Ponytails were good for dogs' ears when she was Underdog and I Sweet Polly Purebred. Beauty arose at age twelve like the anthills I used to step on. Grew also, hardened, unhurtable. The two of you now formed a womb against their freezing, piercing eyes ... too inexperienced to even think of doing anything else but daring enough to do it before everyone.

There were no masks of soberness or silliness. No mannerisms exaggerated. No catch phrases or smooth lines. No stolen looks. No exchange of names. There was just simultaneous staring ... sleeping, consenting, submitting to the waves in the streams. They seemed to float together into rivers, perhaps, candy-filled, memory-haunted oceans.

"Pick up papers," the blue monster told us in Third Grade. Classroom became a colony of insects or a flock of birds searching for tiny pieces of paper, which the rug was trying to swallow up as the earth does to seeds. Jokes aren't remembered, memorable, or significant. Only laughter important now as then as tomorrow.

Cool! The bubbles underwater rose up during the day to become the stars in the sky at night. Yelled to one another but could only guess at what was being said.

A stranger's car whisking past like a broom sweeping up some unimportant mess. Now temporary death. Now a pillow on the whipping post. The two of you were chiseling away from inside the sculptor's rock, freeing creations from it until you would finally find your way out.

The roast beef smell slid down the steps as you lay on the couch watching the Sunday football games. The little disk was a black party of sounds that filled the young house. She Loves You! Yeah! Yeah! Yeah!!! Yeah! Yeah! Yeah!!! Yeah! Yeah! Yeah!!!"

And the same old words come to mind. Happiness, bliss, pleasure, high, wow, great, ahhh!

The two of you lifted your tear-covered faces and stared at each other. Finally, she exposed her thoughts.

— Chardon's always on my mind!

The commercial ended. You bent over to pick the seed up off the floor.

Amen.

Philadelphia 1981.

Backstage

The heavy grey sky made the campus a low-ceilinged theatre in which fog and mist had danced all day. Just now, twilight had taken the stage and whirled its dark cape behind the Gothic towers of Barbelin/Lonergan Hall. Presently, arrogant night would take all it wanted.

Along the downhill paths dawdled small groups of girls and guys. Behind them the fog embraced the lamp light, veiling yet revealing its beauty as the right dress does with the right woman's figure. She strutted past them, exaggerating a drag on her cigarette. Exhaling, she felt like a fairy augmenting the atmosphere with magic clouds of smoke.

Something about the mist and fog made it seem an adventure could begin at any moment. Maybe it was the closeness of all those molecules of moisture — the whole atmosphere seemed a cloud of moisture surrounding her! — but, somehow the atmosphere seemed to have become electric, as if its purpose were to conduct electricity. She could easily imagine bolts of lightning flashing around her — from here to there in any direction, like one of those electricity displays at the Franklin Institute but with herself as the center, the lightning rod.

Oh, everyone look at me! I'm ready for my close up! And, you're not even the star, just playing the wife and mommy! What the actress does.

Still there was something to it. In this atmosphere it seemed at every moment that some-thing was about to happen … as if someone from your past could step out of the mist … as if a stranger in the fog could instantly become someone you know … or someone from your future whom you will know.

What does the poet see walking across campus?

The refrain of her German professor who loved to go off on tangents about Goethe, Heine, German Romanticism, and its *Traumen* …

Das Glück ist eine leichte Dirne …

— Two people walk across campus and see different things. One sees his way to class. The other, the poet, sees something different. What does the poet see?

Heading from the main path toward the stairs down to Bellarmine, she looked harder at the lamps and wondered what the poet sees.

Alongside the evergreens, tulip-shaped lamps … Costumed from another time … Perhaps … but from a day close enough to ours for us to understand … Edwardian? In elegant Edwardian garb.

And this costuming was necessary … Disguise! Why? Because they are Immortals! Immortals contented at their posts along the curving paths! Immortals who do not command nor beckon nor even call … But simply, … provide!

Ha ha! How about that? That is what the poet sees!

She descended the cement stairs leading to Bellarmine. Quiet here now. Not the usual migration of the herds up and down. Someone should do a nature show about the herds all moving across campus ten minutes before the start of class. A guy ahead of her in sweatpants and hooded sweatshirt trudged along with a bag in his hand.

Obviously headed to the gym. What does the athlete see? Challenges ahead? How far is it? How fast can I get there? How do I feel? Is my heart rate where it should be? Kind of cute, though.

And you with your Immortals in lamp costume! And what, pray tell, do these Immortals provide?

Glimpses of the campus ... in careless lightswatches ... whimsically cut, ... patches of grass and ground ... sprinkled with the high yellow and piercing orange of the leaves, a shadowy image of a short fir tree, a black monster's head projected onto the ground through a branchclump nodding in the breeze ...

Finnessy Field. Girl jogging this way. A big guy struggling a soccer field away. You can do it, buddy. She's skinny as a bean already. Isn't that always the way? Slight frame, long arms and legs. Smooth, taut muscles. Blunt hard elbows and knees. The flushed face almost obscuring the freckles. Rhythm of sneaker crunch on gravel of track.

St. Joseph the Worker with his carpenter's square. St. Joseph, pray for me! He could build a theater for you. Who's the patron saint of actresses?

She gently closed the backstage door, wishing not to disturb the performance of the first one-act play. It was a room of whispers. Some lips were moving to fill silences and kill time. Others were bitten, held still.

All getting ready in their own ways. Some being silly to hide their nervousness, others mumbling their lines. A preview of a many-ringed circus. There was a silly little man in a black suit, derby, and walking stick. There was a young lad on his way to work in a factory. There was an obtuse girlfriend and a nagging wife.

The ash tray was next to the little grey intercom. Through the intercom into the quiet room came muffled audience sounds and rehearsed lines. She buried the light of her cigarette in ashes and stared in the mirror on the wall. The nicotine had calmed her a bit, but did not have the usual affect. Her face was ghostly. A smoke ring rose in the mirror in front of her face and disappeared so quickly that she was not sure whether it had been a full ring or not.

After throwing on the faded, flowerprint frock, she stepped out of her sneakers, pulled off her jeans, and stepped into the worn sensible shoes of the aging mother. She wanted to light another cigarette to see if she could reproduce the ring. But there was no time. Funny the way the most ridiculous ideas can seem so important … The face in the mirror pouted like a child and then smiled at itself.

The intercom trembled with applause. Less time than she had thought!

She lit another cigarette. She did need to calm down a little more. She placed the grey wig carefully on her head, adjusting it with both hands. The reflection was immediately older. Tendrils of smoke shimmied toward the mirror's frame. She placed the cigarette in the ashtray and began making herself up. She had to become a lady with a husband and grown son.

Should she go splashing into the world of the mirror!? How the poet bleeds!

Draw the lines just as you did for dress rehearsal. Placing them where they will really be some day? Who knows? You know. This whole performance is really a dress rehearsal when you think about it. A girl becoming a middle-aged lady. Aging myself. Oh, dear, I'm dating myself — aren't I?! Fast forward. From youth to age. Like with a VCR. From the beginning of the story to the end? Exposition to denouement? Moments and I'll be a mother with an emptying nest. Wishes made and wishes thwarted. Five Fs: fruit, fertile, fecund, futile, finale. Skip over the vital stage of love and marriage, the crazy coincidence of meeting and courting, the wild exhausting energizing early days: love and lovemaking 'til floods of desire empty you. Then the smallest unsatisfied drop scalds you on the inside, too hot to stand. Those days with him. Wonder if he'll be here. He said he would come to see it. Mom and Dad will be there. My mother watching me be a mother and a wife.

Skipping over bearing the child, giving birth, a drama in itself in those Edwardian days, raising a child, wondering if what you told him was right, if you had made a mistake, pushed too much or too little ... As if this movie were made by a man. What the actress does. Or a man has the remote control, anyway.

Yes, we're skipping all that. Skipping it. It's already happened. I am she already. Though it is part of who I am. I am the shape shifter going from maiden to mother to crone. What the woman does! Not showing the hot central stage of swelling womb and milky breasts. Skip to motherhood with a strapping son. Then losing him. You're a crone! A crone!

Achone, achone! Unimaginable? Lose your flesh and blood. Lose those years of vitality. That energy that could lift a car or kill a monstrous attacker. Obscure the years of vitality behind makeup. Instead of obscuring age.

Lose his presence around the house. His presence as a constant care in your mind. They must worry about him still and think, "I should do this" or, "He needs that." Phantom cares. And then to remember that he is gone! Oh, God! It's impossible to really know. After all the thought and work and worry ... and nothing. Except the husband standing there, the dumb ox, trying to pretend that it's not his fault.

Husband. Funny how I am desirous of Man. Man in general. Man in general to be lover. To be boyfriend. But Particular Man?! Oh, how that feeling dries up when faced with a particular man! A very different thing. Different thing altogether. I guess guys must feel the same way. Could explain why they are so cold, how they never care about our feelings.

As she applied the makeup to her eyebrows, she was careful to allow her elbow to brush only gently against her breasts. They were feeling swollen and sore now. She was on her way. No chance of fertility bearing fruit this time. Could use a shot of Wild Turkey. Would have to stop drinking. Smoking, too.

Another crackle of applause came through the intercom.

She took another drag of her cigarette calmly, casting onto her face the look of a serious woman, a grown working-class woman whose life had been filled with care but who loved her family, was brave in the face of the routine of daily toil. Taking quiet joy and pride in it. Hating the rich people, probably. Envying them a little but never believing it was her lot to be like them. God and the preacher and the Bible say it and she believes it. Not much questioning of anything. Not even the dumb-ox husband, really. Simple brave life. Kind of stupid, though. Probably wouldn't even be able to smoke back then.

What the actress sees! ...

Why are we wasting so much time on this? Shouldn't we practice some lines? What if I freeze and the lines just won't come out? The others are practicing. What's with you and all this reflection? Is it normal? Is it necessary? Isn't that the mirror's job? Maybe it's just the day, the mood of the day, and of me at this time. This reflective weather.

Time!

Wisps of smoke rose toward the mirror frame as she removed the wig from her head. Young again. Oh, to be young again! No longer she but me. Everything went blank at first. I couldn't remember a thing. Then the first line came to me and once it got out of my mouth everything else flowed naturally. Barely any thought. I went through all the motions out there and hit the marks, barely conscious of the fact that they were watching, barely conscious that it was going on at all and that I was doing it, or if it was even me out there. Then it was over and they applauded. Suddenly I knew that it had indeed happened and that it was time to get off and return to what we had been before, a little deflated, perhaps, pleased yet disappointed that it's over, satisfied to a degree.

But I did feel the eyes. The wall of eyes out there in the dark. Don't know who they were. Couldn't really see them in the darkness. Could not be seen to look, either. Blow the whole illusion.

She lit another cigarette and started removing her makeup. Rehearsed lines and audience responses came through the intercom. She was in a room full of whispers. Some actors were rehearsing lines. Others tried to act silly to kill nervousness and time.

Manhattan 2004.

That You Do Unto Me

Well, honest to God, when I first seen the guy I said to myself, "The next time Brigid points in any direction and says the word 'cute' — I don't care if it's a baby, a dog, a guy, or a duckling — I'm gonna run like hell the other way." 'Cause I'm tellin' yih, it ain't no Prince Charmin' comin' down na block: it's a freak, some kinda Sasquatch ... a Loch Ness Monster for Christ's sake ... or or or or ... a whadeeyihcallit, that dog with the three heads ... Yeah, yeah, Hercules's dog, exactly. Or something outta *Rosemary's Baby* or *The Omen*.

Anyway, God forgive me, but as soon as I laid eyes on him I wanted to run back inside the building which is not what I expected at all, because I distinctly remember ... I deliberately made a point of askin' her, "Is he what you think is cute or what I think is cute?" And she swore up and down sayin' "Believe me, he's what everybody thinks is cute." And she starts tellin' me some story about some new girl comin' up to her and askin' her who the cute guy in Facultative was and how it turned out to be the same Godforsaken loser she wanted to set me up with and she's like, "Don't worry about it. I'm sure you'll like him" bla bla bla — well, you know how she is. So I'm like, "OK, if it's just for lunch and there're other people aroun', I don't care." Well! Let me tell you!! I mean, WU-O!

What? Hold On. What? In a minute — OK? Hello? Sorry about that. She can't stop tormentin' me for a minute.

Anyway ... What the hell was I talkin' about? Oh yeah. So this guy shows up outside the building. He has this long straggly hair and these dark sunglasses on — y'know the kind with the mirrors on them? They always give me the creeps 'cause they remind me of stories yih hear about those perverted guys who go around with mirrors on their shoes. I don't know if it's true or not either. God knows. Anyway, how the devil did I get onto that subject? Oh yeah. He had these queer sunglasses — like some kind of sixties reject. You know me. Mind like a steel trap for things like that. And he had a ratty mustache that really looked like hell and one of those pointy little beards, yih know, those stupid beards like when they have a beard but it's not a whole beard it's just on their chin like he forgot to shave or somepm? Right. Right. A goatee. He had one of those — really looked like the devil. So I'm thinkin' this guy is some kind a druggie wants to take me to a Satan worshippers' party someplace. Seriously. He reminded me — especially with the long hair and the creepy-lookin' beard — he reminded me of that guy, whatsisname, the cult guy who murdered all those people, the Helter Skelter guy? Yeah. Manson. Charles Manson. That's who Brigid thinks is cute. Charles Manson. Ya believe 'at one? She also seems to think it's a great idea for me to have lunch with him on the hottest day in August in the middle of Cen'er City Philadelphia. I mean, yo Brij? What in God's name were you thinkin' about?

Honest to God, I was content to just sit in the caf in the air conditioning. But, no, Brigid and her ideas. "Oh, this new girl came up to me and asks me who the cute guy in Facultative is" bla bla bla. Jesus, Mary, and Joseph, it's bad enough I have to work in the same building with a guy like that but to think that my friend would think I could actually be attracted to a creature like him! The thought of it makes me sick to my stomach.

But you know what was really weird? You know who this guy really reminded me of? The Devil. My hand to God, that's all I could think of as I walked down the street. I was walkin' along the stinkin'-hot Chestnut Street goin', "My friend, Brigid, set me up with Satan." Yeah, right. A real lunchdate from hell.

And if he really is God's Gift than why in blazes does he have to get Brigid to get dates for him? And why does he bring the whole goddamn mailroom along with him? Oh, I di'n't tell yih about that? Yeah. He brought Mr. Mack's kid and a couple of these other fishfaces with him that I di'n't know. Like I say, I was all ready to eat inside in the air. *But!* They said it was some kinda Friday tradition and Marlene was on vacation and I figured, what the heck, mine as well take advantage of it. Well, when I started walkin' with this crew I cou'n't believe it. I thought the sidewalk was gonna melt right underneath our shoes. They certainly picked a good Friday to include me in their tradition. So help me, I swore I'd never be a part of this tradition again.

OK, dammit. OK! I told you I'd get off in a minute.

I'll tell yih one thing about walkin' down the street with a guy is yih don't get all those rude remarks from the construction workers. That was one good thing about goin' to lunch with Lucifer, I guess. I still wasn't too ecstatic about the whole thing, though. Him and his friends were ignorant, too. As we were goin' up Chestnut Street, we came up to one of those strange-o religious fanatics tellin' everyone that the world was coming to an end at five after five. He was handin' out little fliers tellin' people to repent or they would go to hell. Well, he tries to hand some fliers to our little gang and every one of them — the demon, the fish faces, and even Brigid! — blew right by him without takin' anything from him. I was like, "This poor soul is out here on a stinkin' hot day handin' out his little pieces of paper. The least I could do is take one." I glanced at it and then threw it away a half a block later. But, I remember what it said because it got this song from church stuck in my head for the rest of the afternoon, "Whatsoever you do ..." Right. Right. "When I was hungry, you blabla bla bla ..." But the wording of it was weird. Like, some Protestant way of sayin' it. "Whatever you do to my least little ones" or "my little least ones" or somethin' like that.

Where was I? That's right. At any rate, at this point, I was anxious to get to the place if only for the air conditioning if nothing else. At least, I assumed it was gonna be air conditioned. But, come to think of it, I wou'n't put it past this romantic devil to take us to a place without air. I mean, pizza? Yih gotta be kiddin' me. Who wants pizza on a day like today? I woulda been content with a salad or something light. What? Well, I almost did. I had half a mind to, so help me God, a number of times before we got to the place. I was ready to turn right around and march back to the air-conditioned cafeteria. That woulda taught Brigid a lesson about messin' around with other people's lives, tryin' to get people to "try this" or "go there" and "I think he likes you." God save us! She's a real headcase. Honest to God, I don't know how I put up with her sometimes. Her "matchmak*ing*," as she calls it. She always *"ings"* like that. Did yih ever notice? "Matchmak*ing*, meddl*ing*, mak*ing* a fuck*ing* annoy*ing* nuisance of myself!" I don't know. I notice all these things, anyway. Maybe I'm the one who oughtta be committed!

So, anyway, we take a right up 17th Street and we go into this little hole-in-the-wall place. I'm tellin' yih, I could not figure out for the life of me what in the name o' God I was doin' walkin' into a damned place like this. The place is so dark I can't see a God's blessed thing. Of course, Mr. Devil has his sunglasses on and he has no problem seein'. It was so dark in there especially after comin' in from the out of the sun that I coul'n't see where I was going. I bumped right into this fat lady. Really deesgusting. It made me wonder what kind of low place the guy was takin' me to and what kind of common people he likes to hang out with. Of course, the fat deesgusting lady turns out to be our waitress. Not only that but she knows all of these guys. They all said, "Hey, Roz" like they've known her all their life. So, "Roz" leads us to a table in the back. We have to push our way through the biggest crowd of weirdos you've ever seen. There were all these druggies and black guys and construction workers. Yeah, real classy joint. We end up at this table so tiny yih could barely fit a drink on it, for God's sake, let alone a meal. I'm thinkin', "What kind of hellhole is this guy leadin' us into?" I almost left right then and there but I kept thinkin' maybe its not his fault, maybe it's not as bad as I think and I di'n't want to do that to Brigid. Plus, they did have the air on, thanks be to God. Yeah, yeah, that's right. I coulda really used a beer at this point, too!

So, I just kept givin' the guy another chance and another chance, figuring it's just lunch and it will be over soon enough. But it wasn't workin'. The time kept moving so slow and I coul'n't stand the sight of him after about five minutes. I just kept watchin' the waitresses and all the other customers. The place does a good business. I was surprised. I never even heard of the place before today. Seventeenth. Yeah, between Market and Chestnut. It's a real hole in the wall, a total dive. Yeah, and romantic as all hell, let me tell yih.

So, "Roz" comes over with the menus and the Prince of Darkness says we don't need 'em. I almost screamed. How dare he? How dare he say he knows what to order for me without askin' me? So help me, I wanted to kick his shins black and blue under the table. I can make up my own mind, thank you very much. Treat me like that again, pal, and there'll be hell to pay. Believe you me! I'll be damned if I ever let some guy treat me like a child.

Oh, pizza. Pizza and beer is what he ordered for everybody. Nobody else said a word. After the waitress left they all start tellin' me that it's the best deal in the place and they get the same thing every Friday. I smiled and tried to be nice and then I went back to watchin' the crowd. There were some shady looking people in there, believe me. There were some black guys in there trying to sell jewelry. And there were these construction workers comin' in all dirty lookin'. The door kept openin' up every couple minutes.

Oh, one thing I forgot to tell ya. On the way down Chestnut Street, Beelzebub kept makin' all these stupid jokes. I don't even remember what he was sayin'. Alls I know is he was talkin' ten times louder than he shoulda been. I'm not sure. Some God-forsaken place in Southwest Philly. I don't know the parishes down that way. Anyway, he starts doin' the same thing in the bar. He's doin' all the talkin' and makin' his stupid jokes and it wou'n't surprise me if they could hear him back in the office on the 22nd floor. Honest to John, the kids he brought with him di'n't say a word. They just kept laughin' and noddin' their heads.

No, his body wasn't really bad or anything but he was no Mr. America. He was kind of scrawny, y'know?

Anyway, where was I? I sat there and tried to make the best of it. I drank a cold mug of beer and talked to Brigid a little. I was on my second mug of beer when I started to feel more relaxed and I looked at Lucifer again and thought maybe he's not as bad as I'm makin' him out to be. So, Roz comes over and with these little pizzas — y'know, little personal pizzas — and she hands him to Mr. Satan and he starts handin' them out to everybody. The place was so cramped someone had to help out. And as he was handing the pizzas out, some more construction workers came in the door and the room lit up again and I was like, holy shit, now I know why he looked so familiar. Now I know who he looks like and why I kept getting' that feelin' that I should give him another chance. It's not the devil that he looked like: it was Jesus. And if there was any room, I would've fallen right out of my seat. I never realized before how similar they look. I mean, they could be brothers, fer Chrissakes!

Philadelphia, Manhattan.
Completed 2002.

Athletics

— Excellent!

The elevator doors opened wide to welcome Eugene Prendergast into the empty car. A gorgeous afternoon here outside Three Mellon Bank Center. We have first-rate conditions for today's contest, a dry course, mild temperature, and the sky is sunny and clear over Center City Philadelphia. Oh, my! It looks like Gene Prendergast is off to a tremendous start. He's made it onto the elevator alone at four minutes before five — without being seen! What do I need? Gateway's a dollar eighty. Got the buck. Got to change out of these clothes — sweaty smell. Quite a skilled performer. A six foot two veteran of this race. Out of Havertown, Pennsylvania. Been around a number of years but still has many years ahead of him. At 27, many people say he still has his best years ahead of him. Well, you know with great starts like the one he got today I don't know how long it'll be before Gene starts bringing home a few of those championship rings. Let's see, one, two. There's fifty. One, two, three: cool. Fantastic! Eighty cents. Sick of the smell. Monkey suit. Is there another 35? Put that in the other pocket. No, not long at all, I imagine. Not long at all before he's wearing one of those rings. He does have some competition, though. Today's race promises to be an especially hotly contested one. There's that special motivation which comes with a Friday race. Gonzo Friday. It's *great. I can hardly wait ... until the weekend!*

Oh, great!

Prendergast's elevator stops with a jolt and is invaded by two ugly, chubby women, both in their thirties, one blonde with a lot of rouge on her cheeks, the other a brunette wearing dark glasses and an excess of perfume that makes Gene think of purple. They occupy the center of the car. Gene leans against the wall in the rear right corner, affects a look of fatigue and indifference so they won't talk to him, and watches the orange numerals flash in descending order.

— So she was syow trawmatoized she cou'n't come ta work taday.

— I don't understand. Is she movin' far away?

— Nyeow, nyeow. Jus' deyown na shtreet. You knyeow, from one house to dee udder.

— That girl takes a day awff every time she breaks a nail.

— She hasn't had the job teeoo long — has she?

— Nyeow! She just got it. That's why she's such an do-ope.

— She's rooinin' her big chance.

You stupid cows are ruinin' my life. And youse're makin' me sick to my stomach. Man, between the perfume and the gum ... The crowd getting excited now. You can hear them chanting as the elevator brings the athletes to the ground floor for the true start of this contest.

— 17 ... 16 ... 15 ... !

How much effect do you think the fact that it is Friday afternoon has on these athletes, as opposed to some other afternoon or shall I say "evening"? We can hear how it is affecting the fans. Well, you know, I believe it has a tremendous effect on the athletes as far as their getting up and as far as their swiftness and eagerness and the motivational ... Motivationwise, I'd say, "yes" that Friday is the best day to have a race, to watch one, or to be in one. It most certainly does have an effect — and a big one at that. It's a day on which records can be set and broken. We have to remember here that these Racers are not only racing home for the night but they are going home for an entire weekend. They may not be racing exclusively home either. They may be going to their favorite places to eat or drink or watch movies or to a show or a date or a host of other things that these Racers are interested in. Stop at the Manoa for a quick one? Murph's supposed to hook me up. See if he's there? Why not? That's right. Also, they may be leaving the city for the weekend. They may be sick of work and know that all they have to do is get this commute over with and then they have two whole days and a night, which makes it a whole nother thing. Make sure it's just a quick one, though. Wanna change. Eat, too. We'll have to check with the statisticians to see exactly how much time away from work these contestants have. At any rate, it is a very long time. Well, I'd say these runners definitely have something to run for this afternoon. What do you think? I can't argue with you about that. Maybe I should say "evening." Hold on. I think ...

— Ba Bom Ba Bom Ba bombombombom Bom Ba Bom Bom!

Yes! We've reached the ground floor. Rriiiinngg! The doors are open. Gene stands aside for the ladies as specified in the Rules and lets them out first. He then bursts from his inferior position and takes the lead as an experienced distance runner does when, after having kept pace with the front runners, he decides to go into his "kick" and sprint toward the tape. In this case, however, we have Prendergast on his way to the revolving door closest to Fifteenth Street. He easily outdistances not only the others in his car but many of the others as well. We see him zigzagging across the floor of the lobby, a slippery part of the course today — wouldn't you say? Well, it certainly can be but it doesn't seem to be a factor in his performance at all. He handles it quite gracefully as he comes upon a little Oriental Lady headed after the mailman. Should he pass on the left? Right? Left? Right? Left! Good eye, Gene, good eye. He checks his time by the clock at City Hall while negotiating the revolving door. Oh, my! It is not yet five o'clock and Gene Prendergast has made it onto the sidewalk outside of his building! This kid really came to play. He rushed out of there like it was on fire or something. Unreal! Things going remarkably well for Prendergast this afternoon. Funny how they hire all them Orientals instead of the Blacks. What do you mean, "all our employees are white"? Look at all the Chinamen we got. And there's a black woman who answers the phone who sounds white. She is black, though. I can attest to that. The timing is critical here and Prendergast knows it. Oooh! A fine athletic move around the old woman with the cane! He showed good acceleration there as he stepped quickly to the right and then just as rapidly back to his left to gain the lead on the old woman. Marvelous! Should pick up several precious seconds with that. Well, he moves so fast you could easily lose him in the crowd. That's the beauty of watching a contestant of this caliber compete in a race like this. That's why I don't agree with these reformers who say the Racers should be allowed to run through the streets. You'd miss the grace and the athleticism of moves like that. I can't agree more with you on that and you're not even mentioning the safety factor and so forth. The role that both safety and strategy and experience play can't be underestimated. Prendergast, for our viewers at home, with the brown suit and tie and the yellow shirt and let's not forget — mustachioed! His hair light brown, a bit long in back, receding a little on top, kind of pinkish on top from the sun. Look at him go! You know, that is where, motivationally, a Friday race comes into play. Moves like the one he just made, as we said before, show the importance of that motivational factor. The timing is important as well. One second can make the difference between a successful crossing of Fifteenth Street and a disheartening, potentially disastrous delay. Funny way to get around a quota. You wouldn't think it was so funny if they put N.I.N.A. in the window, though — would yih? I guess not. It's really not too cool. It's a big crazy struggle in this country: Chinks, Niggers, Harps, Wops, Whites, Blacks, Men, Women. It's a nuthouse. Makes it exciting, though. Gives it all this energy. And all the WASPs sit back and watch. Telling us what to do while they rake in all the money. Them and the stinkin' Jews. They let us do all the fightin' and they make the profit from it all. What a way to run a railroad, as Joe says. Hey, but they pay me whether I work hard or not. So I'll take their money. Who cares?

We've come to the Street Crossing. The DON'T WALK sign is flashing. Like I said, this can be quite dangerous for the Racers. That's right. You know, this is where that Friday afternoon factor that we talked about previously, negatively becomes a factor once again. The more motivated the runner is — and I think in the case of Prendergast we have motivation which is quite high indeed — the bigger the risks they will take in trying to get across. Though the Friday Factor can help by giving boldness to a performer who otherwise is on the timid side, it can also get that adrenaline pumpin' so high that the athlete runs a high risk of getting into an Error Situation and possibly even a serious injury. Look at that! God! She's nice. Prendergast seems to be admiring a young blonde ahead of him in the crowd. For our viewers at home she's the one with the hourglass figure in the peach top with no sleeves and the short navy-blue skirt. That's another thing that Prendergast has going for him — good taste. I seen her before. Catch her eye today. Maybe Monday see her again. Try to bump into her and talk to her. Hey, stranger things have happened. Maybe run into her again at McGlinchey's or something. Hook up. Hang out with her at lunch time. It'd be nice. Nice blonde. "Strawberry blonde," I think they call it. It would do you some good. That's your whole problem, you know. She's not bad at all — big handfuls, not a bad ass but hard to tell in that skirt. Thick ankles — maybe thunder thighs. Don't matter though, really. Sneakers. Maybe if she had high heels on, her legs would look better. Getting' to know their tricks — aren't yih?

Oh, my! Gene goes to his right along the zebra stripes past the *Triune* sculpture and moves steadily but not too fast against the flow of the automobile traffic. He's all alone over there. He's like a baserunner taking a lead, trying to get a good jump. Yes! He finds a hole between a stopped Chevy and a slowing Toyota and off he goes! Beautiful!

That was something to see the way he threaded that needle, let me tell ya. What Prendergast did in that situation was, you know, he played it real well, not letting the adrenaline lead him into an Error Situation, not letting the excitement take over. He bided his time, moving the whole time toward his goal, not always at top speed but trying always to stay in motion, always moving towards that objective, always keeping that goal in mind — his immediate objective here is the giant *Clothespin* — and not making his move until he was sure there was sufficient time and space for him to pass through. Peripheral vision and knowledge of the course and training ... And don't forget a great deal of good, old-fashioned instinct helps these runners on a day like today. Quite a good performance for Gene. He's ahead of his usual time as we see him hop from the street to the little hill of cobblestones. Actually, we see from his split that Gene is well on his way to running a race that would give him his fastest time, lifetime. He steered clear of that tree nicely. He now is about to enter into the thick of things. He'll be surrounded by men in suit jackets, mostly blue but a few grey and brown ones thrown in. Muscular black girls with big earrings with their names on them will take the field along with some of their male counterparts in Georgetown jackets and their cohorts in Sixers' jackets. Some wear baseball caps. Others prefer the flattop hairdo so popular these days and leave their heads uncovered. Female executives and secretaries hurry toward their destinations as well. Why don't you give our viewers at home an idea of what it is like to be in this part of the race? O.K., well, down there in the trenches, as it were, you have that crush of all kinds of various bodies wearing cotton, denim and leather and lace. You see bra straps and blouses and huge white sneakers. You get the smell of bubble gum, perfume, and cologne, sweat, exhaust, and cigarettes, and hot dogs. That's right. He's also got those vendors to contend with. The vendors cause problems for some Racers — don't they? They do. You know, people underestimate the difficulty faced by these Racers but a Racer like Prendergast faces obstacles that our viewers at home may not comprehend the difficulty of. He's got the vendors who could make a sale of a t-shirt or a soda or a pack of cigarettes or a pretzel right in his path and catch him off guard and have him blocked up for a full second, possibly more for a less experienced Racer. You also have to watch out for the Handbill People. Handbill People can cause a real frustrating Delay Situation. Combine them with a delay from a vendor and customer and you may as well just kiss that championship ring goodbye.

Amazing! Having passed the tree, Prendergast squeezes himself between the t-shirt vendor and the cigarette vendor. He now moves onto the sidewalk, careful not to step on a crack, joining the crowd of pedestrians, running for daylight, flanked by the pretzel vendors on his right and the Continental Bank on his left. You know, that is one of the best things about broadcasting this race from the City of Brotherly Love — those Philadelphia Soft Pretzels! Oh, my, yes! Between them and the cheese steaks I'd weigh more than three hundred pounds if I lived here in Philly! That incense stinks. Tell these turban guys to go peddle that stuff in Ethiopia or someplace. Prendergast, however, seems to keep himself in remarkable shape. And he moves really well for a big guy, you know. Yes, excellent lateral movement, fine agility. Surprising for a man of his size. He tries to go left to pass some Talkers but he's blocked by Jim the Ventman. Where'd he get that bottle of J.D.? Poor soul, always wears that coat, even in the ninety-degree heat. Better than going around with no pants on, at least. Quite an aroma he's got going there, too. What were them three things about springtime? Gene spots an opportunity as the mopey-looking fishface in the grey cap holds up the Oncomers. Who does he think he is — Studs Lonigan? He dodges quickly to the left and then skirts back over to the right. Oh, my! A real close one there for Prendergast but he made it. Did he touch the mopey-looking fishface in the grey cap? I don't know. It's hard to tell from this angle but, you know, a lot of times it is difficult for these Racers, intense competitors that they are, to avoid hitting the passersby. Very often they are tempted to lower their shoulders and knock them out of the way. However, professionals like Prendergast never do such things. These professionals have to deal with unforeseen events like running into the Talkers who don't seem to realize that there are other people in the world besides themselves. They also have to keep an eye out for handbags, briefcases, unexpected changes in direction, speed, or even sudden complete stoppages. Maneuvering around the handbags can be quite difficult, you know. Oh, yeah, and the swinging arms of some bejeweled woman in front of you can be dangerous if they don't know you're coming. That's right. They'll hit you right where you live. A bracelet to the groin — devastating to a male competitor! Look at that one! Look at all of them. That's one of the best things about spring is when all of these beautiful bodies that have been wrapped up all winter are set free and start bouncing up and down the street. Mmmm! Hello. Nothing special about the face but that body is tremendous! Prendergast turns to get a look at the ass of a former Oncomer. Oh, my! All I can say is "Wow!" She's gorgeous in those black-and-white striped pants. I don't know. She's not that good looking, really, but she is sexy as hell. Check out the cops in the Paddy Wagon looking at her. Such cockiness, too. Probably spends more time undressed than she does dressed. South Philly girl. After easily going around the right side of the blonde woman in preposterous high heels, Prendergast begins a post pattern straight for the *Clothespin*. Three signs of spring in the city: days start getting longer, the girls starting looking better, and the city starts to smell like piss. Of course, the Racers have to work on keeping their concentration. Yeah, in case anyone thinks this race is easy, consider the amount of possible distractions that could occur at any time. The Racers can't afford to waste too much time looking at the nipples poking through the tight, red t-shirt over there or the amazing ass in those designer jeans or at the young woman with the brown ponytail and the white bow over there or at that pair of unbelievable legs or those shapely ankles or those swaying hips or that slit skirt or the supple flesh of those long bare arms. Heh, heh, heh, heh. A guy could forget about the race altogether. Dirty old man! A tall, bald, white guy with glasses, a Handbill Person, is distributing fliers directly in front of the steps and right in the path of the speeding Prendergast. Gene slows. There's that chick again. Wow! He allows the young black man with the flat top hairdo to come up on his left and pass him. Do them guys ever buy that incense? I doubt it. Brilliant! The black man stops to take the proffered handbill and Gene is able to go around him and hit the stairway! What a move! What a figure. Hope she's going my way. That's exactly what you could use. She's really beautiful. She could change your life. What is it about her, anyway? I like all that hair, the wings. Get all tangled up in it. It's her shape mostly — them hips swinging. Her sexy wiggle. The swerve of her hips, and the large breasts on that small body. She's hot. Maybe see her on the El.

— Would you like to sit down?

— I noticed you at Fifteenth Street and I wanted to-

— Would you like to join me for a drink? I'm on my way to the Manoa Tavern.

Boy, that'll make her swoon — won't it?

Anyway. Did you see that move around the Handbiller? Astounding! Remarkable! Fantastic! Way above Par! Things are going so well for this young man this evening!

— Perhaps you would care to join me on the 104 bus? You see, I haven't quite gotten the funds together to pay Mr. Costello's fees for the inspection.

B. Dalton Bookseller bag.

— Now, how did the people at your office let the prettiest girl leave without offering to carry that heavy bag for her?

— I see you like to read. I like to read also. What kind of books do you like?

— Novels? I used to read books when I was at the University. Temple 1980. Now, I'm partial to the *Daily News*. Sports Section, you know.

Will you be serious? Think of something. But

they're all stuck up now. It's so hard to find a girl who's interested in what I'm interested in. Not like in the 70s. People partied back then. It was easier. Maybe some other time. It's worth a try. No one since what — January? It would be good for you. Exactly what you need. Oh, leave me alone. It's Friday. You could have someone to meet for lunch. You could call her on the phone at work. Commute together. Some other time. Oh, my! Look at Prendergast go! He's even passing people as he descends the twisting stairs! Unbelievable! Not much difficulty weaving through, making his way down, not using the railing. Keeps his ankles and feet loose. Nice fluid motion. Incredible! This lad moves faster than the mortal eye can follow! Now you've really gone off the deep end. Leave me alone. It's Friday. Take her to the top of Penn Center and look at the city, take her out to Havertown, have her stay over, or to a hotel room here. Could definitely use at least some of that. Give her a ring, have a proud wedding, a honeymoon in Cancun. On the beach with no one around to see or hear. Knock it off. I've had enough aggravation this week. I want to be left alone. That's my motto for the day. It's Friday! Leave me alone! I should climb up Billy Penn's hat and yell at the whole city, "It's Friday! Leave me alone!"

Down here in Penn Center Concourse on the way to the Market Frankford El, this is the real test of a Racer because the patterns of movement are so unpredictable. You don't know where people are going. They're going every which way. You know, I guess it's really not accurate to talk about Oncomers in this situation at all. I mean, everyone is a potential Oncomer. That's an interesting way of looking at it. You've got businessmen and women with their suits and briefcases. You've got the young girls. You've got a guy right here in front of you stopping to light a cigarette. Left? Right. You've got the Hallahan girls still in their school uniforms. They'll be jumping in the fountain soon. You've got the kids from Central and from the Prep. You've got the black kids with their Adidas t-shirts and their boom boxes. All Day I Dream ... You've got bums and derelicts and thieves and Septa officials. You don't know what you're going to run into down here. The key, however, is not to push too much, not to overextend yourself, not to let the opponents force you into making mistakes but to stay within yourself. You don't want to let them force mistakes on you.

The smell of spring is down there as well. That's for sure. Prendergast keeping up with his record pace. He's around the bottom of the *Clothespin* now and making ready for the Stair Leap. He reaches into his left pocket and up he goes! Did you see the way he hurdled that first stair, hit that middle stair with his right foot, and bounded over to the newsstand in a single stride? Now that is athleticism at its finest. Yes, and the way he handed the man the thirty five cents — the thirty five cents he got ready during the elevator ride, if you recall — with his left hand and took the *Daily News* with his right hand. That's the kind of thing that just can't be taught. We hope the youngsters were paying attention to that play. Really shows the way the game should be played. Exact change and everything! We're watching an artist this afternoon, a real master! Shouldn't we call it "evening"? Folds it and places it under his left armpit. Now for the turnstile. Turnstile coming up next and Gene is there.

This could be another Delay Situation. Strategy and experience and split-second-decision-making qualities are really needed here. A competitor has to know which turnstile to choose. *Have fun in the city!* Gene on his way to the far left turnstile, the one nearest to the WESTBOUND TRAIN ARRIVING sign. *My girl, she's so pretty!*

An elderly black man has dropped his coin. Looks like a quarter! Probably needs it for the dollar-twenty-five fair. It's kicked by a wealthy passerby right into Gene's course. Gene sees it, scoops it up like a shortstop, and:

— Sir! Sir?

Old guy, hard of hearing. Not even looking for it.

— Sir!

The old man gave him a suspicious look.

— Sir, I think you dropped this.

— Oh, yeah?

Whiskey.

—Yes, I believe I did. Thank you, son.

He put the quarter into the old man's hand.

Fine display of generosity there by Prendergast. That's right and you know I don't believe it cost him a thing pacewise or timewise. It's good to see that sportsmanship still hasn't gone totally out of the race. *Tonight, I'll lose my bread! Tonight, I'll bla bla bla whatever!*

Gene now joining the line of commuters waiting to pay their way on to the El. He should sail through smoothly. That blind lady again. She's always down here. How 'bout that guy kickin' the old guy's money and not even stoppin'?! He had real short hair. A clean face with no worries. Probly comes from money and's got plenty of his own. I can't stand them. Probly on his way to the Paoli

Local to his big house on the Main Line. They're the worst of them all. You won't see him on the Jungle Bunny Express. That Todd trying to tell me what to do! Well, think again.

Haven't you and your ancestors started enough trouble on this planet? Imagine! Starting your own religion and then trying to force it on people in your country and on every continent on the map practically! I don't think there's a continent in the world that they haven't carved up for themselves. White Man's Burden. Well, fuck you! I know there's a lot of room in hell for guys like that. If there's an ounce of justice in this universe, then hell's gonna be a regular old WASPs' nest! And he can say "hello" to Lord Mountbatten for me while he's down there.

What is taking so long? Here we go. Anyway ... Gene at the booth now. He's in a hurry. He hears the bell and sees that the WESTBOUND TRAIN ARRIVING sign has blinked on. Hurry up! The woman in the booth has not given Gene the go-ahead and, boy, you can tell he's not happy about it. Commuters are arriving at the top of the stairs, apparently having gotten off the westbound train. A man tosses his lit cigarette on the floor. Come on. Fat, lazy, good-for-nothing! Go back to Africa! I wish they'd all go back — on a boat with a hole in it! I don't know why they do that, those Fare Collector Officials. She sure is a fat one, too. Let the power go to their heads, I guess.

— Gateway, please! Yes, a dollar eighty. That's what I gave you!

Animal!

— No wonder they keep you in a cage!

Apparently there's been some kind of an altercation,

some kind of altercation going on between Gene and the foul-mouthed Fare Collecting Official. Don't read lips, folks. Must not have been moving fast enough for Prendergast. He is through the turnstile, though, and the green Gateway transfer is safely in his right pocket. Tempers do flare in these races, you know. Intense competitors like Prendergast can easily lose their cool. Especially on a Friday race. Really! I don't have to put up with that today. I don't know what her problem is. Just 'cause she's in a bad mood, just 'cause she's got to work, doesn't mean she has to abuse her power like that. She doesn't have to take it out on me. I don't need to be cursed at by that gorilla. Move, Lady! Gene can't seem to get around the two heavyset black ladies at the bottom of the stairs. They're engrossed in their conversation. Oblivious! Come on! Move your big fat butts for once in your life! Apparently, they're in no hurry. Too late. The El has left and Prendergast hasn't even gotten to the platform. He's still on the blue stairs as the El leaves the station.

A boat with a big hole in it! No food over there anyway. I'm tellin' you. One of these days I'm gonna kill one of them big fat slobs! They are the most selfish, the laziest, most cowardly race on the face of this earth! And my Wage Tax goes right into their Welfare checks so they can buy grape juice and junk food. Standing there talking like there's not a soul in the world besides them two! No consideration for anybody but themselves. It's their city, though. You have to admit that. It belongs more to them than it does to you. Well, they can have it. The animals are running the zoo and they've already set it on fire. Too bad they didn't burn the whole Goddamned place down. I'm glad I don't live here. Inconsiderate cows! I ought to throw one of them on the tracks. Look at them! I've seen cattle with more intelligence in their faces. It doesn't make much difference anyway. I might not have made it. That's right, you know, Prendergast hasn't really lost any time. With the jump that he had on the competition, that El may have gained a false sense of importance. It is still quite early and if he had not gotten the head start, then he wouldn't have even seen that El. Another one should be along shortly. You're right. He still is way ahead and he's still running a personal best time. Besides the 104 bus doesn't leave until five thirty. We can understand his frustration but he shouldn't let a minor setback dampen an otherwise stellar performance on this Friday afternoon. With the exception of the single elevator stop, the slight turnstile altercation delay, and the Talkers at the bottom of the stairs, everything has been going Prendergast's way today.

You've got what it takes. Salem Spirit. Hotter than I thought. Lots of sweat. Spiders crawling down my back. The kid in the Adidas shirt lights a cigarette. All Day I Dream About Sex. They love that Menthol — don't they? Gene on the platform close to where the front of the train pulls in. Already preparing for his exit at 69th Street. *Share the spirit. Share the refreshment.* He'll most likely be entering through the front door of the third car. He can hear more Racers putting their coins in the change box and coming through the turnstiles. He begins to get anxious. He wants to get going. He does not want to lose his lead or to squander the good fortune he's had thus far. Wait a minute. The light on the far rail of the westbound track appears to be lengthening. It appears to be brightening. Gene casually moving over and stepping on the yellow caution markers, leans out over the tracks and peers both between and around and above the heads of the others who, like himself, missed the El only moments ago. There is a light in the tunnel. Yes! The next El has left 13th Street and should be here any second. The light on the tracks grows brighter and brighter. Quite a stroke of luck for Prendergast. Despite missing the earlier El, he's going to get on another one before the throngs of slower nine-to-fivers come to join him! He should make the bus easily but, perhaps, we shouldn't speak too soon. No, please don't jinx me. There she is on the other side. Northeast girl. She's got a nice face, only a little makeup, blue eyes, not too hard lookin' for the Northeast. Young. Should have talked to her. She's cute. I never had a chance. Too bad she's wearin' them sneakers. She could look a lot better. Should have said something. Maybe you'll see her again. Keep an eye out for her. Sure, always some other time. Look, it's Friday. All I want to do is sit back, relax, have a few beers, and watch the Phillies beat the Mets. I don't want any aggravation. I don't want any pressure. I don't want to have any silly conversations with some stupid secretary from the Great Northeast — O.K.? I just want to relax and enjoy myself. Is that too much to ask? Probly should've. Never had a chance. Shut up. Here comes the El. *I'm not waitin' for a lady! I'm just waitin for the El!*

I'm really getting thirsty. We'll be at the Manoa soon. Have one or two and then go home, eat, shower, change out of this monkey suit. Don't forget about Murph. He said it was "The Killer." Wraps are in my wallet. Listen to the roar of that train, Ladies and Gentlemen. Check out the way Prendergast doesn't even flinch as it pulls into

Fifteenth Street. Only, one or two though, chief. How long do we have? 48 hours to Sunday and then twelve 'til five in the morning: 60. Plus four equals 64 hours. 64 hours our statisticians tell us. Those are the hours away from the office that these contestants have from Friday afternoon until Monday morning and with which to do whatever pleases them. You can tell Prendergast is anxious to get on that train and get out of the city. His head, his mouth, his throat, his heart, his very veins cry out for the first cold beer of the weekend! He's seen too much of this place, same old office, same old corner, same old El stop, day after day. Weeks, months, years pass without an iota of change in the routine. But we've made it through the week, thank God. Thank God it's Friday. That's for sure. Many Racers come hurrying up behind Prendergast but Gene boxes them out for position as the El train comes to a halt. That's no easy task. These people are quite competitive. The El hisses and its doors slide open. Oh, quite a move! Prendergast is the first one in!

The car is not very crowded and yet Prendergast is unable to find a seat. Stand next to where these black women are sitting. They'll be getting off first. Can you see her? Her train is coming. Too late. Missed her. Gene decides not to read his paper for the moment as we can see. Instead he stands there looking at his reflection in the dark window and glancing at MacGruff's urging him to take a bite out of crime. This El train is a B. There is no air conditioning on these trains, you know, and let me tell you during the summertime races all those fans do is blow the body odor around. Did you know that this is the longest stretch that the Market Frankford El goes for without stopping? I never really thought about it but I guess you're right. We've gone by the 22nd Street stop of the Subway Surface Line and now we're under the Schuylkill River. In a matter of moments we'll be entering 30th Street Station.

It looks like Gene's play calling is paying off here. As we pull into 30th Street Station, the woman seated closest to Gene and wearing the fancy sunglasses stands and heads for the doorway. Gene steps aside but does not move back. Well done. That way he doesn't leave an opening for someone to take the seat from him. The other woman still seated and wearing the big earrings gives Gene a threatening look and with little dignity begins to move her buttocks onto where the woman with the fancy sunglasses had been. Oh, my! Did you see that? Prendergast! With the seat! Refusing to be intimidated, he does not flinch, does not give in to those intimidational tactics. Despite her trying to slide over, giving Gene no room, and her giving him an upward wary glance filled with nastiness and contempt, despite her affecting a lack of caring by making her face look like a dog's when it takes a shit, Gene takes the seat. Note the subtle use of body language by both the woman defending the seat and Prendergast. Note Gene's aggressive posture in response to her Decoy Nonchalance Move. And something very important perhaps even all-important here and that is his lack of hesitation. He goes for it right away. Boom! The defender has no choice but to back off. She never had time to gain territory. If he had taken a moment to think about it, he probably would have lost the seat. You can't give them people any indication of weakness. If they push you, you got to push them right back. Otherwise they'll walk all over you. You can't be nice to them. That's just the way they live.

You can't give them an inch. If he had waited a second or two more, she may have had her buttocks spread across the entire seat and Gene would not have been able to take it without a nasty confrontation and perhaps a violent struggle. He'd be standing reading advertisements for sore feet instead of reading the sports page on a cushioned seat. He probably would have missed his opportunity, if he had waited. However, Gene possesses that rare combination of experience, instinct, and knowledge that makes a great athlete.

The combination most of us know simply as, "talent."

With a capital "T." Oh shut up. Shut up and read.

At 34th Street Prendergast takes note of his fellow passengers. Along with the business crowd, he sees three skinny kids at the far end of the car, St. Joe's Prep students most likely, with maroon jackets that are too big for them and too clean. They must be freshmen. They're talking and giggling among themselves. Another older Prep kid sits by himself. I'd stay away, too. Them kids are embarrassing, real goofballs. A wrinkled old black man in a dark suit and tan cap nods off in front of Gene. He gives off the smell of vodka. His watch says it is five oh four. Halfway down, the black boys in baseball caps point at him and the girls in huge earrings with their names on them laugh out loud at the sleeping drunk.

Nearing 40th Street! Couple getting ready to get off. College kids probly. Penn kids. Both dressed the same — denim, carrying them backpacks. Prendergast observing some youngsters from the University of Pennsylvania. The girl has light brown hair, shoulder length and has those wings again. Her face is fair and cute but like a statue, stony-looking. She has a pink Oxford shirt under her denim jacket. She is pretty rather than sexy. So is her boyfriend. He's pretty like some teenage heartthrob you'd see in *Tiger Beat* or something, same chiseled features. They both display some colorful buttons — yellow and green and red. "END APARTHEID NOW," they say.

I don't know about these kids. I guess they can tell you about Africa or whatever but ask 'em about West Philly and it's like, "Sorry, I got a paper to write." What is that Apartheid, anyway? Why is it so popular all of a sudden? Some African thing. They should be more concerned about the Blacks here. I mean, that blotchy skin and ashy dryness can be a real bitch. Oop! There they go. Off to make the floor sticky at Doc's or Pagano's or Smokey Joe's. I'm sure they can't party like we did in the 70s. We were crazy. Oh, well.

Crazy old lady with black and grey hair. Seen her before. Always gets off at 46th Street. Must still live down here. Talk about the hardheaded Irish! Now that's crazy. Prendergast not too into reading this afternoon — is he? Well, that's another effect of that Friday– Shut up. Maybe I should say, "evening." Enough!

Prendergast spots the bright blue of the station sign and he knows he's reached 60th Street. Soon the El will cross the border and we will no longer be in Philadelphia. Gene stands to let the woman with the big earrings out. The train has no more black passengers now. This is our last stop in the City of Philadelphia. Gene checks his pocket. The Gateway transfer is still there.

As we pass by the 63rd Street station — remember

we don't stop there on a B train — Prendergast tucks his newspaper under his left armpit again. Newspaper maneuvering is paramount to good racing. One wrong move and you could put an eye out. Will you knock it off? I can't help it. This stuff keeps coming out. Can't wait to get to the bar so we can shut you up. Yeah, then you'll have to listen to the real thing. Are you kiddin? You love it. This is better than Monty Python.

Some people get off at Milbourne and go to their cars, which they parked for free. The rest, all Caucasian, make ready for the final leg of the race — the Terminal Run. As the El comes to its final stop, Prendergast is standing by the doors like a racehorse before the starting gates. The train wheezes and the doors slide open. Gene races — the Contestants may run at this point since we are no longer on the street — toward the P and W stairs, a favorite shortcut of his, scales the stairway two steps at a time, and sprints through the terminal to the suburban bus platform to catch the 104.

So quiet in here and the air feels good. This rumbling could put me to sleep. Prendergast now seated on the right side in the very back of the 104 bus and is awaiting its departure from the terminal. A beautiful girl with a sandy-colored ponytail, pearls around her neck, in a black-and-white-check, spring dress, and, who is standing, it seems, anxiously, by the back door of the Media trolley with a seemingly weightless black handbag dangling from her shoulder, appears to have captured Gene's attention. A tall, narrow-shouldered man in a grey suit (probably with a name like "Brad") and with perfect hair greets her with a kiss. She smiles with delight and the two disappear into the trolley car. Watching a girl like her going away and knowing you'll never know her, never see her again is just like being punched in the stomach when you're not ready for it. Man, it's been a long time. "I just want to be friends." Give me a break. Is that the bus driver? No, just another gray-haired guy with a briefcase and a trenchcoat. Oh, God, when will I be able to get out of this rat race? Why? Is there something wrong with the Facultative Department, something wrong with being where every boy dreams of being when he grows up? Maybe I'll hit the number. Either that or I'll end up a hunched over skeleton working for coolie wages like old Mr. Mack. What's going to happen? There's just a long dim hallway ahead of me with Mr. Mack standing at the end of it. What am I going to do? Find some idiot girl in Havertown? Doesn't look good. Hook up with one of them bimbos in the business suits at Houlihan's? Right! I'd rather go out with a mannequin. They're so fragile it seems like one touch and they would completely fall apart. They deserve to get it with a pool stick. A mannequin would be more of a real person, too. I can't stand those ugly business suits they wear. And they even wear ties, gigantic flowing bow ties. Can you believe that? Imagine! Volunteering to wear a tie when you don't have to! Wanting to be equal with us is one thing but do they have to start dressing like us, too? Stupid bimbos! Sometimes I wonder ... Let's get going, dude, or it'll be 6 o'clock before I get a beer. Who's left? The secretaries and their whining and their bubblegum. End up like Bill and Donna, bunch a screaming brats and a mother-in-law and no money. Here comes the bus driver.

Cool!

Well, it seems that it is time to say goodbye once

again. The 104 bus is climbing the hill beyond State Road and, before we know it, it will reach Pica's and Cawley's, the AM/PM and St. Lawrence's, O'Malley's Restaurant and Costello's, and the Hilltop Diner, where it will enter the 33rd County. From there it will proceed to MacDonald's, Emmet's Deli, Dunkin Donuts, and, ultimately, and, I'm sure some would say, finally, the Manoa Tavern. Prendergast has shown finesse, skill, consummate sportsmanship, endurance, and talent during today's race and, as he puts his head back to take a well deserved rest, we should say he is clearly the winner of our contest this Friday evening. Also, you know, we shouldn't forget to mention that Anheuser-Busch, once again, proudly names Gene their Budweiser Racer of the Week. This Bud's for you, Gene Prendergast! Anheuser Busch will be making a contribution tonight to your favorite charity, which just happens to be Budweiser Beer. And, please remember, no broadcast or copies of this telecast can be made without the expressed written consent of Philadelphia Racing and the National Racing Council. Any unauthorized use of this telecast is prohibited by Law and violators will be prosecuted and locked up in a boat with a big hole in it. So, once again, thank you for joining us. And, until Monday, I'm Joe Loudmouth. And I'm Harry Talkstoomuch signing off. Have a good weekend everyone! We'll see you next week! And the crowd goes wild!

— Excellent!

The doors of the bus opened and Eugene Prendergast stepped onto a corner of the intersection of West Chester Pike and Manoa Road. Much of his life had taken place around this intersection. Sacred Heart was right down the street: there with the school, the annex, the kindergarten, and, of course, the church. He had gone to that school every day for nine years if you included kindergarten. He had received the sacraments at that church — Baptism, First Penance, First Holy Communion, Confirmation. He still went there once a week to hear Mass in that old stone building. 33rd County, indeed. Hilltop Country Club was behind him. That was where he had gotten his first job, as a caddy. That was where he had entered this rat race. The first beer he had ever had was drunk on that golf course. It had been obtained illegally from the Manoa Tavern just across the street. Gene entered the bar and as his eyes adjusted to the dimness of the lighting, he chose the first stool that he came to, hung his jacket on it, and sat with his back to the door.

— Yo, Gene.

— 'ey, 'tsup, Steve? Whaddaya say? Workin' hard or ... ?

— Hardly workin', I guess. They ain't exactly bustin' the doors down yet. Draft?

— Please.

Gene removed two five-dollar bills from his wallet and placed them on the bar. Steve was a stocky little guy with a broad happy face and a full head of thick brown hair.

— You're here a little late again — aren't yih? Still ain't got the car fixed?

— No. I still don't have the money. I was kinda hopin' Costello would let me slide but he won't.

— What is it? The alternator?

— Yeah. It's not that big of a deal. I just gotta get the money together. That's all.

— Pain i' the ass.

— Really.

Steve put four ones, a quarter, and a dime in front of Gene. The bartender wore his usual blue and yellow rugby shirt with his jeans and white sneakers. "The bumble bee look," Gene called it.

— Yeah. I don't mind takin' the El so much but once I get to 69th Street I wanna get in my own car. I don't want to have to deal with Septa anymore.

— How do you like ridin' with all them niggers, though? I thought the El would be the worst part.

— They don't bother me most of the time.

— If I 'as down 'ere everyday, I'd carry a blade or somethin'.

Gene gulped at his beer. It was almost finished.

— It ain't bad durin' rush hour. I'm used to it. I just gotta get money to get the car fixed so I don't have to take that damn bus all the time.

— If you ain't got the money, yih ain't got the money. 'nother one?

— Sure.

Gene finished the beer and slid the mug toward Steve. After bringing Gene a full mug and slapping another thirty five cents change on the bar, Steve wandered toward the back room with an empty bucket. Gene turned his left wrist up and unbuttoned his sleeve. He rolled it up over his elbow so that it wrapped tightly around his bicep. Murph wasn't there. The bar had only one other patron, an old man slumped on a stool directly across from Gene's. Sparse and unkempt grey hair surrounded the pink bald spot at the crown of the old man's head. He was gazing downward at the lazy triangle formed by the ashtray, the empty shot glass, and the half-filled mug of beer before him. A weary cigarette burned in the limp right hand that he rested on the bar but he made no effort to lift it to his lips. He didn't drink. He didn't speak. He didn't move. Breathing seemed a strenuous activity for him and he seemed to do little of it. Gene undid his other sleeve and rolled it up. Steve returned with a bucket full of ice.

— Been down na Bothy lately?

— I ain't been 'ere since 'at night two weeks ago. The night I seen you there. The night we seen the blind lady. You?

— No. I haven't been 'ere since 'en either. I see that blind lady all the time, though. I saw her today, actually.

Gene blushed.

— What's 'at?

The sound of the ice falling into the basin had drowned out what Gene had said.

— I said, "I saw her today."

— Oh yeah?

— She's in the same spot everyday.

— Yeah?

— Yeah, she's always in the Concourse. You know where them stairs are across from City Hall?

Steve examined the ceiling for a moment. Then he squinted at Gene.

— By the place where they sell the hot pretzels, Gene added. You know, near the stairs ... Not the escalator but the stairs ... near the escalator ... right across from City Hall.

— Oh, yeah, yeah, yeah, yeah. I know where you

mean. I know where you mean now.

Gene looked down at his beer and dropped the subject.

Steve sauntered out of the room again with his empty bucket. The beer tickled the back of Gene's throat, cooled and soothed his dry esophagus, and, as it made his way into his empty stomach, gave him the feelings of warmth and relaxation for which he had longed. His eyes, while avoiding the sight of his own reflection in the mirror behind it, traced the line of liquor bottles over to where the old man took a quick, grotesque slurp of beer before slumping over again. Above the old man, a woman pantomimed a rock stage show on T.V. She was running around in a pair of tight shiny pants, playing a bass. It was not plugged in. Gene looked away. His eyes ranged over the jukebox to the empty chairs and tables and lingered upon the old, faded photographs that hung at a distance on the wall. He knew by heart the features of Philadelphia's former athletes of renown: Richie Ashburn, the Whiz Kid, Chuck Bednarik, football's last Sixty-Minute Man, Wilt Chamberlain of the Warriors. Closer to him were some clippings documenting the Phillies' last World Series win from newspaper issues he could still remember. The papers had started to yellow. His eyes finally came to rest on the diamond-shaped rack of baseballs and the sets of old, wooden Adirondack bats affixed on either side of it like several sets of foul lines.

The woman on the television squealed:

— I want to be your baby!

— Just wants to be my bimberina, Gene mumbled.

— You got that right. She's got that covered, I

guess, Steve responded, turning around with his full bucket of ice and looking up at the T.V. screen. I don't know what kind of bass playin' she does like that, though.

— All these girls do is shake their asses in front of the camera. They're so full of themselves they don't even know what they want. I hate this crap.

— Oh, I don't know. I don't mind it too much if some chick wants to shake her ass in my face. I kinda like it, matter of fact.

— Still doesn't make her a musician.

— Who cares? I just turn the sound down and look at the pictures. Look at her! She just wants to do my ... Ha ha ha ha ha! Steve dumped the ice into the basin.

— They don't even know what a dick is. They deserve to get it with a pool stick or a baseball bat if you ask me.

Steve wasn't listening. He was waving his tongue at the screen and laughing. In a moment he turned back to Gene disappointed.

— This one ain't really that good lookin', though.

— No. I don't understand why this one's popular at all. I hate all this disco stuff. I thought we got ridda that a long time ago. Music's gettin' to be a waste a' time anymore.

The old man let out a horrifying cough.

— Hhhiiiieeechch!

— There's still some good stuff aroun'. Ja hear Yes got back together?

— What're they called now? The Front? The Firm?

— Yeah, The Firm. Like the place you work for. Prendie at The Firm!

— They're ah'ight. I can't get too excited about

them, though. I wanna get tickets for Robin Trower next month. That should be excellent.

— Definitely. I hear Zeppelin's gonna be down JFK. I wanna see that. I ain't seen them in years. Phil Collins is gonna play drums.

— Yeah. I'm there for that, too. Incredible! Ten years ago we had Led Zep as the number one group. Now look at what we got! Bimberinas dancin' around with no clothes on. What a difference!

— It sells, yih know. What do you want? It beats lookin' at you all night.

Gene laughed. It was time to drop this subject, too.

— Not much to look at in here tonight. 's 'at guy ah'ight over there?

He was slumped over putting out his cigarette.

— He's O.K. He'll be goin' home soon.

— That cough is somethin' else.

The sound didn't seem to belong to this world.

— Really. He's in here almost every day. He'll be gettin' his second wind in no time. You watch. Never has much to say for himself, though.

They fell silent for a moment. A commercial for acne medicine played on the screen.

— Should be some chicks here later on tonight, Steve announced.

— That'll be cool. I hope they don't come too early, though, and take over the place. I wanna see the game.

— Bet you got some nice ones down Center City. Them secretaries an' shit?

— Oh, yeah. Definitely, we got some nice ones but most of them are either married or stuck up. I don't know.

They all got a bug up their ass. They all want some rich, up-and-coming businessman. I don't like going out with someone I work with, anyway. After you break up with thum you gotta deal with thum every day. Too much of a hassle.

— If I 'as down ere I'd be like. "Hey, honey, I might not be rich but I'm definitely up and coming!" Heh, heh, heh, heh!

Gene blushed, pretending to laugh.

— I can't imagine you working down there, Steve, he said.

— I can't imagine doing that everyday, either. I can't picture myself wearin' a business suit to work.

— Anyway, them girls in town working in them offices are so stupid. They don't understand that workin' sucks. For some reason they think the business world is glamorous or somethin'! I just don't get it.

— They been watchin' too many movies.

— Yeah! Or too many soap operas or somethin'. And they ruin all the bars downtown. Like Houlihan's and shit? All them places got D.J.s on Fridee night and all they play is that teenybopper stuff. And you know the only reason they play that stuff is to get the girls to come.

Steve snorted.

— Damn straight!

— And the faggots that hang out there with 'em are all such a bunch of hypocrites. These goddamned yuppies, they're like, "Yeah I think you're equal to any man and I admire you and respect you as a professional" when all they're interested in is gettin' into their professional panties. It's just disgusting. They're all completely phony — the guys and the girls. They make me sick to my stomach. That's why I don't hang out downtown after work.

The old man wheezed and coughed as if his throat and lungs were about to give way.

— And them people can't drink neither, the bartender said. The chicks always order them fruity drinks or these things with so much juice and shit in 'em that they don't even taste the alcohol.

— Yeah! They always order these red drinks and these green things with umbrellas in 'em an' shit. Then they have one of them and they're wasted.

— Them dudes ain't much better. They have two beers and they're on their ass.

— You watch, though. Someday these workin' babes'll be beggin' to stay home again. After they figure out it's not so glamorous. They'll probably call that a revolution, too.

— No shit.

Sunlight teased the corner of Gene's right eye as the door behind him swung open.

— Pren-*DEE!* What's happenin'?

Before Gene could turn around to see who had entered, he was slapped heartily on the back.

— Coll', you asshole, how y'doin'?!

Gene and Coll shook hands by intertwining their thumbs, a soul shake. Steve pulled a mug of beer and delivered it to Coll who remained standing next to Gene. Gene pointed to his money and told the bartender to take it out of there. He handed Steve his mug after finishing off its contents.

— So, Coll, seen Murph' around?

— He ain't been in here? I was hopin' he'd be here by now. He's supposed to hook me up.

— I just got here and I haven't seen him. Thanks, Steve.

Steve gave Gene another beer as well as the change for the drinks and headed for the back room without the bucket.

— I seen him this afternoon. He was goin' to see the Colonel and then he said he was comin' here. Cheers.

— Cheers.

— I was supposed to hook up with him, too. Hopefully he'll show up soon.

— Well, I gotta split, Prendie. I can't really hang out. I just wanted to see if he was here. The wife's got dinner cookin', y'know.

Coll smiled as if this were a running joke between the two of them and Gene tried to smile back. Coll polished off the mug of beer.

— Tell Murph I was lookin' for him, he said.

— Ah'ight. Be back for the game?

— Yeah.

— Cool!

— Later. Thanks for the beer.

— Take it light.

The sounds of distorted, electric-guitar chords filled the room and, onscreen, an astronaut stood on the moon by a flag that kept changing colors. Steve, returning with a case of Budweiser bottles, stopped in his tracks and stared up.

— Coming up in the next hour we have videos by Frankie Goes to Hollywood, Animotion, and Loverboy. But right now ... !

— Yo, Steve! Will yih-

He didn't hear him.

The T.V. showed a blonde woman in a strapless, red dress. A pulsating beat thumped from its speaker. The blonde seemed to be imitating an old movie as she squeaked.

— Turn that shit off — will yih, Steve? I mean, gimme a break.

Steve put the case of beer down on the bar and picked up the television's remote control. He was kind of amused by Gene's annoyance. He pushed some buttons and the familiar theme song to Action News triumphed over the silence of the room. It was six o'clock. Gene looked at the screen without really paying attention to what was being reported. There was something about hostages and a hijacking in some backward country. People were ranting and raving about the MOVE fire and some rowhouse in North Philly was shown burning. He just wanted to see the sports. Steve started to shove the bottles of beer he had into the cooler near Gene.

— So, how's work treatin' yih, anyway?

— Ah'ight.

Steve apparently wanted to talk.

— We're not real busy these days. Things have settled down a little. I'm busy but not overwhelmed.

— How do you like workin' down 'ere? Like I say, I can't see myself doin' 'at.

— I have trouble dealin' with it myself. I look at myself in the mirror sometimes and I say, "Who is that guy in the monkey suit?"

The old man reared his head and stared in Gene's

direction. Gene noticed his gaze, met it for a second, and then looked back at Steve. He continued:

— I hate wearin' these clothes. I'd rather be in a t-shirt and jeans playin' ball all day! Or, hell, I'd rather be drinkin' all day for that matter.

— I can imagine!

The old man rose from his seat and limped toward the Men's room.

— Are you sure that guy's ah'ight? He sounds like he's gonna die over there.

— Yeah. I told you. He's in here all the time. He's a nasty old fart. Retired Philly cop. Corbett, I think he calls himself. You couldn't kill him if you tried. He'll be fine. He's part of the regular lineup around here. Believe me. I'm surprised you ain't seen 'im before.

— No. I haven't.

The old man came back and sat down. He appeared much more alert than before.

— I'd rather be playin' ball all day, too, Corbett rasped.

Steve and Gene glanced over at the old man but found him slumped over. Neither of them made a reply. From the T.V. overhead, the gentle holding forth of the newsman continued. Gene had gotten a look at old man's face. Something about his features, maybe the man's long pointed nose and deep-set dark eyes, made Gene think he looked like an owl.

— So, Carlton's pitching tonight, Steve remarked.

— Yeah. Should be a good one. Doc Gooden against Carlton.

— I hope they kick their asses. I can't stand those Mets.

— No, me either. They're a bunch of pretty boys, not real ball players.

— I'd rather be playin' ball all day too, the old man grumbled.

Steve started to turn his head around but stopped. Gene adjusted his behind on the stool. The two friends' voices grew louder.

— What about Schmidt? You think he'll do anything tonight?

— I don't know about him. He'll probably strike out all night, knowin' him.

Steve, to Gene's great disappointment, put the last bottle from the case into the cooler and left for the back room with the empty box.

— Don't you think I'd rather be playin' ball all day too? The owl-faced man shouted.

Gene raised his mug. He felt sorry for the old man but he really didn't want to talk to him. Maybe he would change the subject. He cried out:

— Well, I'm glad it's Friday!

The old timer also raised his mug. They drank. The old man then wheezed and cackled strangely before his laughter disintegrated into another coughing fit.

— Friday? He said when he recovered. Friday? I drank with you 'cause Friday means somethin' to youse kids but it don't mean nothin' na me. Friday don't mean nothin' na me no more. See, I'm retired.

Old Officer Corbett was very drunk.

— It must be nice to have all that free time, Gene

replied, trying to feign enthusiasm.

The old man cackled again. He moved as if he were starting from a nightmare.

— Must be nice havin' free time! Must be nice havin' free time! I got time but I ain't got the body to do anything. When you're young, you got a strong body but you ain't got the time. You can do things — play ball, dance, make love to a woman. Me? I can't do nothin'. But I have the time. I got nothin' but time. Nothin' but time. Nothin'!

— I know what you mean. That's the irony of life, Gene said politely. When you have the ability, you don't have the opportunity. When you have the opportunity, you don't have the ability.

Steve came back with another case of Budweiser bottles. He placed it on the bar and began loading the bottles into the cooler.

— Nothin'!

Steve looked over at Gene and shrugged. He had never heard the old cop rasp on at such length.

— Steve! called the owl-faced man.

— Yeah?

— I'm gonna buy this young college man a beer. Give 'im another one on me.

— Thank you, Gene protested, but-

— Don't mention it, son.

The old man collected his cigarettes and his matches from the bar and rose from his stool. He almost knocked his beer mug over when he went to pick it up. He started to move toward Gene. Gene grew nauseous. Corbett wore a dark blue rain jacket that had wet spots on the forearms, a white wrinkled dress shirt, grey flannel trousers, white socks, and black loafers. Gene felt trapped. Only vicious rudeness could keep away the old cop. The man sat down next to him. He reeked of body odor and whiskey and cigarettes. Steve brought Gene a full mug and picked up the owl-faced man's.

— So, you from the Main Line?

— No.

— Aw, c'mon, c'mon, c'mon, c'mon, c'mon. Where yih from? Where yih from? Ah, Rosemont? Villanova? St. David's? No. I know where. Rosemont! Rosemont? Are you from Rosemont?

— No! I live right over on Wils-. I'm from right here, Manoa.

— Yih did go to college, though — dincha?

Gene nodded.

— See? I knew it. I knew it. Listen, listen, why ja come here, anyway?

— It's Friday!

— Hhiiiieeech!

Spasms of laughter and coughing overwhelmed the old cop. Gene watched with alarm as the man's owl face scrunched itself up into a mass of reddening wrinkles. After a moment the old man recovered and continued:

— That's right, Friday. Heh, heh, heh, heh.

— Yeah, answered Gene, somewhat offended. I ... uh ... It's Friday night and I just finished work. So I'm havin' a few beers.

Corbett leaned in close to Gene. The stench of whiskey filled Gene's nostrils, overpowering, for the moment, those of body odor and cigarettes.

— I heard you talkin' about a game. You playin' in a game tonight.

— No, no, no. I'm gonna watch the game — the Phillies and Mets.

— Watchin'. Watchin'! I know all about it. I spent all my life watchin'. I'm a retired Philly cop, y'see. That's why that Friday stuff don't mean nothin' to me no more. Nothin'! I'm retired. You know what I mean? Come to think of it, that Friday stuff di'nt matter much to me when I was on the Force, either. Sometimes my Friday was a Wednesday morning! Hhhiiiieeechch. Heh, heh, heh, heh. That's 'cause I was a cop. Now, I'm not anymore. I retired. But I used to watch a lot. I used to get paid for watchin', watchin' everything, watch traffic, watch cars, watch people. I always had to watch. Thass why I don't watch no more.

Gene gulped down some beer. He was getting lightheaded and weak. The beer seemed to be coating the lining of his stomach with warmth, emphasizing that there was nothing inside it. It was a familiar feeling. He knew it was hunger, but, with the odors of his new companion's wretched body, his whiskey, and his cigarettes nauseating him and with the glasses of beer he himself had drunk masking it, the sensation was different than the hunger he felt during the week. He wanted out of this situation but what could he do? He was trapped. It was just like being in his office at quarter to five.

— Watchin'! I hate watchin'. You like watchin'. I know what you like. You like to watch the girls — doncha?

Gene smiled.

— Oh, once in a while. Yeah.

Steve swaggered out of sight with two empty cases

and reappeared in a few moments laden with two full boxes.

— I don't watch. Well, sometimes I watch, you know, outta habit. All them years on the Force. I watch people. You ever play ball, son?

On the television the sports segment of the news was ending. Gene was losing his patience.

— Huh?

— I said ... I said, "Do you ever play ball?"

— I used to play softball on Sa'urdees but I'm not playin' this year.

— You're watchin'.

— I'll probly be sleepin'. I don't know. Maybe I'll go to a few games. Why?

— I used to play ball when I was your age. Are you a cop?

— No.

— In my day, God, we played ball all the time. Me and all the boys in the precinct.

— A young cop like you, you oughtta play. This time a year–

— I'm not a cop.

— Well, whatever you are, yih should be playin' baseball. Thass what I say.

— I just ... I don't know. I lost interest, I guess. A couple of the guys got married. I don't know. The fun went out of it.

— The fun went out of it. I know. I know. That happens. Well, lemme tell yih, the fun goes outta this, too.

The owl-faced man pointed a bony finger at his beer mug. He paused. He grabbed the mug and knocked back the rest of the beer in it. In the midst of his forecast, the Action News weatherman giggled with the anchorman and the sports guy. The old man's mug slammed on the bar. Then Corbett tried to get onto his unsteady feet.

— The fun goes outta this, lemme tell yih. I'm gonna get outta here. I'm gonna get outta here before this place fills up with youse kids with your game watchin' and your girl watchin'. Do you have a wife, son?

The old cop flopped back down on his stool as if it were crucial for him to obtain this information before leaving.

— No. I'm not married.

— Do yih got a girlfriend?

— Not right now. No ... I ... I don't have one.

— You watch girls, though — doncha?

— I guess I do.

Corbett nearly rose from his seat again.

— Well, why doncha talk to one of 'em? Instead of to old farts like me?

— Well, I'm here for the game. If somethin' happens, it happens. If not–

— I got a woman at home. I don' unnerstan youse kids today. It's won'erful havin' a woman around the house. We have our fights. Sure! But we make up. That's the fun part. Hhhiiiieeechch. Heh, heh, heh, heh. She's home waitin' for me right now. She's probly like a hornet's nest — angry as hell. She's a real hellcat. She's the one who wanted to move out here. Well, she shoulda known better than to marry a Kensington boy. You can take the boy outta Kensington ...

Gene had a hard time believing that the man was actually married. He felt obliged to have the owl-faced man's mug refilled, nevertheless. Gene held up two fingers.

— Steve! Two more, please.

— Thanks, son. But after this I gotta go. The wife's waitin', y'see.

Steve eyed Corbett with suspicion but filled his mug anyway.

— She's probly madder than hell. Women are won'erful. You may stop watchin' your games and settle down. It may be sooner than you think. The Force is not a bad way of life and you get a good pension, lemme tell yih.

Gene glanced up at Steve and shrugged. He kept quiet.

— I know. I know. I know youse guys. Think they'll never get married! But you mark my words. You mark my words.

— You may be right but–

— An' before you know it, you'll have a baby on the way. An' when a woman is pregnant …

The retired cop held his hands in front of his paunch. Steve leaned back near the cash register and watched some of the national news. Some terrorist thing was on, same footage that had been on the local news.

— When a woman is pregnant, God, thass the mos' beauteeful thing in the world. They think they're ugly but they're the mos' beauteeful thing in the world. When the woman is pregnant with your child? An' when the child is born? Boy! Lemme tell yih: it's a miracle. When the kid grows up, you teach it. You're the most important teacher. The parent is the *most important teacher!* You teach discipline. You teach the kid to play ball. It don't matter if it's a boy or a girl. They got girls in Little League now. You play ball, son?

— I used to play softball but I'm not playin' this year.

— I see. Oh yeah, yeah, yeah. A couple of the boys got married and you don't play no more. In my day, everybody on the Force played. I played ball. I played, boy, lemme tell yih. Third Base, the Hot Corner. I played in grade school. I played stickball, halfball, all kinds of ball. I played high school ball. I played American Legion. I played in the Service. I played with the boys from the precinct. I tell yih anytime there was a game goin' on, I was there. I played, boy, and lemme tell yih — those were some of the best times. Out there in the sun, y'know?

The old man looked up at the ceiling, closed his eyes, and felt the warm spring sun caress his twenty-two-year-old face. He gestured with his cupped left hand from the bar to his pointed nose.

— An' the smell. You know. The smell of the grass. The smell of the fresh grass in the spring ... like now ... or maybe a coupla weeks ago. The smell, boy. You know that smell?

— Sure.

— Of course, you do. Of course, you do, the old man slurped. You know the pleasure of the game.

While pushing his chin down to his chest, the old man stretched out his right arm and shook his finger at the display of baseball bats on the wall.

— Hittin' the ball with a good wooden bat! Yeah. Excuse me. Yeah, I can tell. You know the pleasure of the game. You know the pleasure of playin' on a spring day. Baseball and fallin' in love — that's what the springtime is all about. Me! I can't do neither of them things. Mine as well be win'ertime all the time for me. Springtime don't mean nothin' to me no more. But I had my day. I had my day in the sun, boy. I had my days of playin' ball and hittin' and runnin' and racin' around. I had my spring days and nights with my wife. You gotta learn them things, son. You gotta learn them things. Speakin' of the wife, I gotta go. Thanks for the beer, kid. They usta call me "Wiz," y'know, like a Wizard, only for short. That was in my ball playin' and courtin' days. I was a Wiz. I was a Wiz. Next time you see me, you call me "Wiz."

Gene shook the skeletal-seeming hand of the old man and watched him stumble out. Before the door swung shut, a smooth, full-fleshed hand, small, feminine, and ringless, grabbed it and began to pull it back open. The brief sunlight in the threshold revealed a pretty blonde woman and then disappeared. The door of the Manoa Tavern closed behind her. She was alone.

Miraculous!

She remained near the door, trying to search the room with eyes that hadn't yet adjusted to the dimness. She wore a red t-shirt and faded Levi's. Her white sneakers shifted around nervously. She sighed and started to turn back toward the door.

— Can I help yih'?

— Oh, no, not right now … Well, …. actually, do you have a payphone I can use?

— Here, said Steve, placing on top of the bar a white plastic phone with a peeling faux-wood sticker. Use this one.

— OK, thanks! I appreciate it.

She slipped around a stool, dropped her pink pocketbook on top of the bar, and punched numbers on the touchpad. She wasn't much over twenty-one, if that. Maybe it was just her hairstyle that made her look so young: straight down to her shoulders with a single ponytail, tied with red plastic baubles, disappearing among the free-falling locks. Her shoulders were strong and robust, her frame slender but wiry. She must have played sports.

— C'mon over. Ah, don't gimme that. It was your idea to meet here.

Canned voices on the T.V. erupted in joyful song:

— The PENN-syl-VAN-ia LOT-ter-YYY!!!!

But Gene was entranced by the voice of the young woman on the phone. Warm and soft, it cast a spell of stillness over him.

— No, no, I already ate. Just for a little while. We can head somewhere else later. OK, OK, ten minutes? I'll see yih then.

She hung up the phone and Steve came over to take it.

— Can I get yih somethin'?

— I'll have a Coke, please. She sat down.

— Just a Coke? Not drinkin' tonight?

— I'll wait 'til my friend gets here. She's around the corner. She told me to meet her here but, of course, she's late. I'm makin' her watch the Phillies game for a little while. She doesn't like baseball but she said this would be a good place to watch.

— Yeah, sure. We'll have the game on in a little while. Stay here. We won't bite. Lookit Gene here in the business suit. He's almost respectable.

Gene chuckled.

Over the insistent, perky music, the deep-voiced announcer called out the last of the winning numbers. Gene pretended to be watching the floating ping-pong balls being chosen. Steve placed the Coke on the bar and the woman began fishing through the pocketbook on her lap. Her nose was little and cute, its rounded end turned up an almost imperceptible degree. All her features, in fact, appeared small and girlish. She wore only a little makeup and all of it served to highlight her deep blue eyes.

Steve waved his hand at her.

— Don't worry about it.

— Are you sure?

Steve scrunched up his face and nodded.

— Thanks! She cried and took a sip through the straw.

— So does your friend come in here on Fridees?

— She says she hasn't been here in a while but she used to come here a lot.

— What's her name?

— Joanne.

— From Saint Dot's?

— Yeah.

— Did she useta go out with Mike Fitz?

— Yeah, but that's ancient history.

— Yeah, yeah. I know her. I ain't seen her in a long time.

Steve turned to Gene, seeing his glass was nearly empty.

— 'nother one?

— Nah. I think I'll just finish this one for now.

Steve knitted his brows at Gene, opened his eyes wide, and then turned back to the woman.

— So who do you like?

— Whaaeet?

— In the game tonight? Who do you like — the Phillies or the Mets? The bartender continued.

— The Phillies, of course! See?

She sat back and with both hands pulled down her t-shirt so that it became taut and so that Steve could read the word "Phillies" emblazoned on it in white.

Gene admired the way the middle part of the team name swelled and expanded over her breasts. She had a good figure. But then he lowered his head: he didn't want to stare. The owl man had left a box of cigarettes and a pack of matches on the bar. Though Gene couldn't see her, he could feel the woman's presence in his guts. His right hand toyed with the cigarette box. He wanted to call out to her, something casual and witty, something noncommittal. She seemed so approachable. But he started feeling sick to his stomach and sapped of his strength. He couldn't think of anything to say.

— I can't stand the Mets! she exclaimed and a flush came to her cheeks.

— I don't blame yih, said Steve as he leaned back by the cash register to watch T.V. Bunch of pretty boys, not real ball players.

The music from Jeopardy rose and fell from the other end of the bar. Gene always said that tune made the contestants more nervous. He looked up at the screen. The host had begun chitchatting with the players. Out of the corner of his eye, Gene could see her take hold of her straw and plug its top hole with her index finger. He gulped at his beer; it was almost gone. He wiped his mustache with the back of his hand. She bounced her straw on the bottom of her glass and then swirled the ice around with it. When she was finished, she lifted the straw above her lips, removed her finger from the top, and allowed the soda she had trapped to fall into her mouth. The contestants on T.V. chose categories and provided questions for the answers.

Gene polished off the rest of his draft. Steve came and picked up Gene's mug.

— No, no, Gene protested, not right now.

He dropped the cigarette box and the matches into the right pocket of his suit jacket, and, taking the jacket from the back of the stool, stood up to go.

— Where yih goin'? Steve murmured.

— I'll be right back. I'm gonna run over to the Westgate and get a Hoagie or somethin'.

The clock behind the bar said quarter after seven. Gene figured the actual time was probably between five and ten after. He left a dollar bill on the bar and took the rest.

— Really?

— I got about a half hour — right? I'll be back in a minute.

— Yeah, Steve shrugged. 'At seems about right.

Gene almost forgot his *Daily News*. Seeing the woman watching him, he gave her a shy smile.

— Be right back, he said to Steve and dashed out.

The sun closed Gene's eyes. A veiny pink shade was all that he saw for his first few steps down Manoa Road toward West Chester Pike.

This is a good idea. I need a time-out so I can regroup before going back in there.

He struggled into his suit jacket, switching the newspaper from one hand to the other and back, and opened his eyes. A 104 bus dropped a few commuters off on the corner. A young mother with her son in a stroller and a dog met her husband and they strode off together along the Pike. On Manoa Road, cars inched forward when the traffic light on the Pike changed. Gene shoved the paper into his left armpit and ambled to the corner.

It'll be much better. Yeah. It'll be much better after I eat. I'll feel stronger. Too much of a buzz in my head now. Whatever happened to just one or two, chief? I don't know, man. They're like peanuts. I'm too weak to talk to her now. Too out of it. She is cute, though, and I don't have much time. Murph's comin' too. Maybe I can go back now and buy her a drink. Talk about the Phillies. I should go back. I should go back.

He stopped on the corner. He watched the young family come to the end of the ThriftWay parking lot and turn right. Gene reached into the right pocket of his suit jacket. He took out and opened the Carlton 100s box. There was one left.

But wait a minute. She's not drinkin'. She says she's not gonna be drinkin' 'til her friend comes. Get her to start now — when she's with you. What'll I say? Her friend'll be there in ten minutes. Less!

The sun made him weaker and more disoriented. He wanted to just lie down on the bench and go to sleep. He was beginning to sweat. Gene lit the cigarette, tossed its empty box toward the trash basket, and missed. He made no move to pick it up.

She likes the Phillies. Just say something about the Phillies.

— So, you're not a Mets fan?

— No, I'm not. Are you?

— No, I'm a blonde fan.

No, no, no, no ...

— I am a diehard Mets fan, myself. Not really. Jus' kiddin'.

You should have made some kind of comment about the Mets. That was your chance. Forget it, now. But hold on a second. Hold on. My head was still spinnin' from that Wiz character. I wonder if he was retired. He didn't mention that, I don't think. Now she's got her friend comin'. I should go back. After I finish this smoke. What'll I say? Right after this smoke I'll go back. What about Murph? Wraps? I got 'em. Don't worry about it. What the hell do I say? And what about the rest of them — Coll and Hynesie and Duff, Defeo the Dago, Mike Doc, Tony Del' (if his wife lets him out), and that school teacher guy, Jack Perry? Maybe Jack'll have some if Murph' don't show. Go back and talk to the girl — will yih? Right! And say what:

— I just went out for a smoke and now here I am back to seduce you?

Is that what you want me to say? And what'll she say:

— Sure thing, dreamboat?

I can't go back now. It'll be way too obvious if I come back with no food. Oh, lighten up. Just say you decided you're not hungry. That's way too obvious. What'll Steve think — that I chickened out when I first had the chance and now I'm gonna try my luck in round two? Who cares? Are you kidding? Come on: she's really good looking and she likes baseball and having fun and all. And she just came walking into your neighborhood bar — by herself! Whatsa matter with you? You gotta go back. But what if it doesn't work? Then what? Let's go eat. This cigarette's making things worse. I'm really spinnin' now. The Pike is spinnin'. It's gonna wrap itself around my brain. It's hot, too. I oughtta eat. Yeah. I'm weak. I should eat first. Oh, I don't know. What a pain in the ass! Unreal! Why did he put this into my head? Now he'll expect me to make a move. The Wiz would be disappointed. Well, we can't have that now — can we? We can't go around disappointing the owl-faced old toads. He called me "son." Incredible! Why'd he keep saying I looked like a cop? Must be the mustache. And who's Steve, anyway? Just a bartender. Yeah, and a friend you've known since kindergarten! It's embarrassing. What'll I say? I know he'll watch everything I do. Or don't do. This is crazy. What am I worrying about all this for? Why don't I just do what I came here to do — get something to eat and watch the game? That owl man screwed me up. He did have a point, though. What the hell do I try to achieve? What do I pursue? I exist at work. No more than that. I gave up softball. That girl is probably sitting with somebody else by now. You missed your opportunity. Just like everything else. I'll be old and drunk and tellin' people, "I never did this. I never did that. I sat behind a desk all day and behind a bar all night." Go back. Go back, man, and give it a try. You'll think of something. Play it by ear. This is your chance, your day. It's been since January. Make a move or stand on this corner all day smokin' the old man's diseased cigarette. The old fool! Probly still thinks I'm a cop. God help poor Mrs. Corbett! I couldn't believe that one. These things are long. They smoke for a long time. Come on! O.K., let me finish this and I'll see.

The cigarette created a floating, spinning sensation in him. His head grew lighter and lighter. He couldn't think straight. Cars sped past him. Nervous nausea gripped his stomach.

I should eat. I really should eat. What am I gonna do — say:

— It's nice talkin' to yih but I'm afraid I'll get too drunk and throw up all over the place if I don't go outside and eat?

I won't be no good to anybody if I don't eat. If you really wanted to meet her, you'd go back right now. It's out of the question, man. I don't know why you do this to me. It's out of the question. I'm gonna go eat.

Gene jerked himself around and tossed the smoking cigarette butt into the gutter. The young family with the dog was out of sight by now. He watched the familiar cracks in the sidewalk pass beneath him as he charged past the pharmacy and the pet supply store. When he gazed upward he saw swinging in the breeze and still nearly half a block away the large yellow-and-brown sign that read: "Westgate Pub." He stopped, thought for a moment about returning to the Manoa Tavern, turned his shoulders as if he were going to do so, and then continued toward the Westgate Pub with more determination than before.

It's the bottom of the ninth with two out, buddy. Get in and out of this place fast.

Gene pushed through the door marked "Take-Out."

Three people were ahead of him at the counter waiting for their orders. Gene sighed with relief. He squinted up and scanned the menu above the head of the young man working the cash register. It was Little Hynesie. A cheese steak would probably take too much time. The smell, however, was enticing. The aroma of steaks and onions on the grill made Gene's stomach rumble with anxious, exquisite hunger. A row of Wise Potato Chip bags, each with its own enlarged dark eyeball, stared with uniform stern expressions at the left side of Gene's face. Little Hynesie wrapped up a cheese steak in white paper and shiny aluminum foil, dropped it quickly into a bag, and collected a bill from a young guy Gene had never seen before. He made change, placed it in the waiting man's outstretched palm, lifted his head and eyebrows at the woman next in line, and asked:

— Help yih?

He wouldn't know me, I guess. Same freckle face. Ask 'im if Hynesie's comin' out to the bar. Nah. A cheese steak'll take too long. Get a hoagie. How 'bout her? She's pretty nice. I'll take one of those please. Aw, but the long-haired dude beat me to it. He's got his hand all over her ass. Get a hoagie. There's no time. Man! Who needs all this pressure? It's Friday, after all. Shut up.

Behind the counter on the wall to Gene's left hung a clock nearly identical to the one near his desk at work. It was twenty-five minutes after seven.

— Shit!

It's not possible. It's over. That's the final gun. The game is lost. We can't possibly order a sandwich, eat it, and get to know that girl before her friend gets there. It can't be done. That's it, pal. The fat lady's done singin', the referee just counted to ten, and you're out. Hang it up, dude.

Gene forgot his hunger. He was enraged at himself, at the old cop who started the whole thing, at everything … His dry mouth and throat complained bitterly of neglect.

The couple took up their food and drink and, arm-in-arm, stepped around him.

— Help yih?

— Oh, … yeah. Hold on a second.

Gene held up his right index finger and marched over to the cooler behind him and to his left. He grabbed a cold, forty-ounce bottle of Budweiser. He got his change from Little Hynesie and stormed out.

Gene headed to the left, in the direction in which he had seen that young family going, and walked away from the Pike across the Westgate's parking lot. He ducked through a whole in the fence that had been there as long as he could remember and found a spot where he'd be hidden from the eyes of the Havertown Police, the spot he and his friends had called, "Frankenstein Alley," when they had been little. He pulled the bottle out of the brown paper bag and flung the bag onto the gravel at his feet. He twisted the cap off and guzzled the beer with four long, furious lifts of the bottle.

Within a half an hour, the sky began darkening. One more swig of beer remained in the unwieldy bottle. Stepping backward toward the rear wall of the Westgate Pub, Gene swallowed the final drops of beer, making sure that not even the smallest bubble was left over, and glared barbarously at the white wall about ten yards in front of him.

Prendergast fades back. The crowd going wild. He's got plenty of time. He spots his receiver downfield ...

He cocked his arm behind his ear and then he heaved the bottle with all his bitter might at the wall. The missile flew in a perfect spiral. Some twilight sparkled on it as it spun. There was a crash when it struck the wall, followed by the gentle, tinkling sounds of the fragments of glass falling on the grey gravel.

— Excellent!

The Bronx 1988, Manhattan, Staten Island 1991.
Revised Manhattan 2007.

Chances

Isla. Santo Domingo in the summer time. Her skin looking so brown in her yellow bikini. Maribel collecting seashells at the edge of the sea. Hair black. Wet only at the ends. Hanging like seaweed down. The blue of the ocean like the jewelry of the Indians. What is it that they call it? Turquoise. Green ball. Red ball. First one red? Yes, red. Red, green, red, green, red, green. All across the ceiling to the other wall. Red, green, red, green, red. *No completa.* Next row. Coming back red again. Red, red, green, red, green. Cockaroach down there. On the mat where Pat walks. Now he's through the hole, underneath. Cockaroaches. *El Bronx.*

Pat thumped a full bottle of Budweiser on the wooden bar and snatched away Fernando's empty.

— Now! he said.

He took a step back and, without seeming to look, he selected the Jack Daniels from the rows of liquor bottles before the long, dull mirror and deftly poured a perfect shot of sour mash through the spout and into Fernando's thirsty glass.

— There you are, Fernando. *Feliz Navidad!*

Gone before Fernando could respond, the bartender glided straight over to the narrow exit at the opposite end of the bar. Una laughed as she heard him singing under his breath..

— Can you hear the drums, Fernando?

No one could appear and disappear like Pat. He was

the reason most people came to the Shamrock. Pat had learned to move well in small spaces. It had been eight years since he'd arrived at Dirty Nelly's fresh from Dublin and indignant that there were no bed-and-breakfasts around Fordham Road. He flew around the corner, passing on his left the small table where cold cuts could be plucked up with a white plastic fork, placed on a Kaiser roll or some rye bread with tart brown mustard spread by a white plastic knife, and taken away on a paper plate with some potato chips or pretzels on the side and a napkin. Pat swung around the back of the pool table and brought forth his cue from the rack. John Malone stood by the right corner pocket at the front end of the table, chalking up and waiting, the bright jukebox blinking behind him. It was Pat's turn.

John Malone could not look at Pat without recalling the bruise his friend had given him on the arm. That John's parents came from Mayo had made no difference. All that had mattered was that John had been born in Liverpool and that England had lost the football match to Ireland. It was surprising the strength the small dark-haired man with the black mustache possessed. He was a good half foot shorter than John and he did not have a muscular build. John supposed he was the wiry sort.

His turn completed, Pat cruised around the back of the pool table, between the complimentary food and the bar's rounded corner, through the narrow entrance, and directly to Una's glass sitting empty in the middle of the bar.

— Another Vodka and Orange, Pat, said Una O'Dowd in an accent stronger than his. She refused to call it "Screwdriver" like the Yanks. It was one of her small ways of maintaining her identity while out here.

— Now, Pat cried, a Screwdriver for Una and a Dewar's on the rocks for Franklin.

— T'ank you anyway, Una crooned, rolling her eyes and examining the molars on the left side of her mouth with the tip of her tongue.

— Always glad to be of service, Una. Any time. The bartender smirked at the bottle of Scotch he was tilting into Franklin's glass.

Gratefully accepting his drink from Pat, Franklin Henry used both hands to slide his full cocktail glass and his coaster closer to him on the bar. He did not want to drip whiskey or ice water onto his grey suit.

— Goin' home to Philadelphia for the holiday, Franklin? The bartender asked. It was funny to hear the name of his hometown stretched out and distorted by his Irish brogue.

— Yeah! Franklin replied with pleasure. Headin' home to West Philly. Lookin' farward to it.

Franklin thought it would be nice to get away from the sound of Spanish for a few days and to stay in a place where people lived in houses with porches instead of being piled up on top of one another. He pictured the rows of three-story dwellings with their covered porches, their hilly yards and their hedges, and he felt happy. Maybe he would stop in at the Cherry Tree Lounge or have some barbecue at one of those smoky little joints on Baltimore Avenue. He could hear the sound of trolleys humming and clacking down the street ... He watched the Market Frankford El thump by and flash like lightning in the distance..

Una lowered herself from her barstool and allowed

her black high heels to carry her clipclopping to the jukebox across the cold, hard, lusterless floor. Bending over to read the listings, she tugged her white sweater with the embroidered pink and yellow flowers over her acid-washed jeans. She brushed the wings of her bottle-blonde hair away from her eyes, but she didn't really need to look at the number. She punched in her selection and her heels took her clopping back to her seat.

She is a pretty girl, but is hard to see her. It is dark. Always it is dark in the Shamrock Pub. And never busy. Only at 4 AM when all the other places are closed. Then the bar is filled with Irish accents. They come also from an island. *Pero fria. Pero Catolica.* They make the bars that are the best: filling up the place at 4 AM with all their talk and smoke, no room at all in here. All the Fridays and Saturdays. These Irishmen, they are the white people who are crazy.

Fernando heard a familiar whoosh. Through the door's diamond-shaped window, he could see a man' s head covered in kinky dark hair. A current of cold air blew in from Kingsbridge Road. Jimmy Santos followed it. A folded newspaper under the left arm of his leather jacket, Jimmy stepped methodically into the room. Jimmy always moved as if everyone on the bar were looking at him. It was as if he were in a game, playing shortstop, and the bleachers were right there. But only Fernando and Pat saw him enter.

— Jimmy, you're late, reprimanded the bartender from over where Una was sitting. Jimmy strode toward the bar. He chose to stand two empty stools from Fernando.

— It's past eight o'clock. What's the matter with you? Pat continued, now directly in front of Jimmy. The open bar only lasts until nine. Look at Fernando. He's been here since half six.

— Pat plunked a bottle of Bud down before Jimmy Santos and produced a clean glass.

— Thanks, Pat. Merry Christmas.

— Merry Christmas, yourself.

Fernando's empty beer disappeared and was replaced with a full one. His shot glass was refilled, and again the bartender vanished. The chorus of Una's song played on the jukebox. On his way to the pool table, Pat unconsciously sang along.

— I told you so! I told you *so*!

He knew every song on the jukebox forwards and backwards, so he said. Jimmy lay his folded paper down and leaned a leather forearm on the bar. He looked to his right, nodded a greeting to Franklin, and watched Pat sink a striped ball in the side pocket. Jimmy mechanically looked to his left, where Fernando caught his eye.

— 'ey, Fernando, he said without feeling. How ya doin'? He smiled about something as he raised his glass to his lips. After a small sip, he set the glass down on its coaster and scanned the columns of classifieds.

Kingsbridge Road sent another gust of cold air into the room. Unzipping their down jackets as they swaggered in were Monaghan and McKenna, the only Jet fans in a bar that rooted for the Giants. Monaghan was the young-faced one with short blonde hair. He was a small, solid fellow. McKenna was big and heavy. He wore his brown hair long and had a thick brown beard. They had gone to Hayes together, Class of '76. Monaghan carried mail, out of the Post Office up in Woodlawn. McKenna now worked for Con Ed.

— Hey, Pat! Where's the free beer? What's goin' on around here? McKenna hollered, flipping a brown lock away from his left eye.

Monaghan grabbed the stool next to Jimmy Santos, leaving McKenna the one next to Fernando.

Pat darted from the pool table, popped open two Bud bottles under the bar, and handed them without glasses to Monaghan and McKenna.

Monaghan said "Merry Christmas" and shook Pat's hand. McKenna shook Pat's hand and said "Merry Christmas." McKenna clinked bottles with his old friend, Monaghan, and Monaghan clinked bottles with McKenna. Noticing his neighbor on the left, McKenna called out heartily to Fernando:

— Fernando! How's it goin'? Merry Christmas, guy! He clinked his bottle against Fernando's glass of beer. Monaghan nodded and performed a toasting gesture from afar. They all drank.

— There's plenty of food over there, lads, said Pat who had suddenly materialized again before them. Youse shouldn't let it go to waste. C'mon, Fernando, Jimmy, eat up!

Winking at Monaghan and McKenna, he added:

— Even Jet fans are allowed a sandwich.

— Sounds good to me, Monaghan said.

Monaghan and McKenna gulped a second time from their bottles and headed without hesitation to the food table. A moment later, Jimmy Santos followed. Fernando watched Pat serve drinks to Franklin, Una, and her quiet friend, Kathleen, who had red hair and freckles. Reaching underneath the cash register, Pat located the controls to the jukebox and turned it off. Happily, Pat inserted the Christmas tape into the box at the far end of the bar. A string section introduced a traditional melody and then the sound of a boys' choir could be heard in the Shamrock Pub. In his best gurrier Church Latin, Pat crooned along:

> — *Adeste fideles*
> *Laeti triumphantes*
> *Venite venite*

— What'sa mattah, Fernando? McKenna, his mouth full of ham, American cheese, and Kaiser roll, asked his neighbor. Eat up, guy! Good stuff. San'wiches ... chips ... pretzels ... 'uh?

He shoved three-fingers-full of potato chips into his mouth.

— C'mon, don't be beahshful, he urged. It's right at the end of the bar.

Fernando nodded. His unsteady feet brought him all the way to the pool table but when he got there, he saw Pat bending over to take a shot. Una' s quiet friend, Kathleen, was out of her seat and standing beyond Pat. The way to the food was blocked. Fernando swerved over toward the rack of pool sticks, followed the far wall toward the crazy door of the Men's Room and hurled himself through it. Always the same smell in here. What they use to clean this floor? **BRITS OUT!** Faucet always drip ... drip ... drip ... *Loca* door. They never fix. Old man in a suit. A girl who work here sometimes. What her name is? Tickets. They are selling tickets.

Fernando ambled past the jukebox and returned to his seat. Next to his beer and shot glass lay a red ticket: KEEP THIS COUPON. The old man was talking.

Monaghan and McKenna turned away from their paper plates to hear what the man had to say. Poppy seeds, crumbs, and bits of potato chips were all that remained on each plate.

— ... our regular customers to a Christmas Party each year. We, the Roach family, wish all of you ...

Fernando could detect traces of an Irish accent. He had seen the man before but he could not remember when. The way he talked reminded him of chanting in Church. It made him want to sleep and dream of Maribel and seashells by the edge of the sea. Fernando looked again at the crumbs on the two paper plates. He had forgotten to get some food.

— And now, as is traditional each year at the Shamrock Pub ...

The music is nice.

We will bring him silver and gold.
We will bring him silver and gold.

No one playing pool.

— Does everyone have one?

The old man put his hand into an old army helmet and stirred something around.

— Now, my daughter, Mary, will do the honors ...

Mary is her name. Mary.

Fernando could see Mary's large red turtleneck and dirty-blonde hair as she went to her father's side. Mr. Roach held the helmet six inches above Mary's forehead. Mary reached her hand inside and smiled with big dimples at the crowd. Kathleen and Una giggled together, red tickets in hand. His ticket on the bar in front of him,

Franklin Henry sat in silence.

Jimmy Santos kept his ticket on top of the classifieds so it wouldn't get wet. John Malone leaned against the darkened jukebox, looking at the ticket in the palm of his tight hand. Frank Monaghan and Joe McKenna faced away from Fernando and waited ...

— And the number is oh twunny nine, Mary called. There was a brief murmur and then everything was quiet.

— Oh twunny nine, Mary repeated.

Mr. Roach took the pea-green ticket from his daughter's hand.

— Does anyone have the number: Zero, Two, Nine? he intoned.

Monaghan and McKenna conferred with one another, shook their heads, and turned toward Mr. and Mary Roach. No one seemed to have the number. Monaghan spun around on his stool and elbowed his friend.

— Hey! Fernando Valenzuela, he shouted past McKenna. Whaddayou got?

— Lemme see, McKenna said to Fernando.

He reached past Fernando's drinks and picked up the red ticket.

— Oh twunny nine! Fernando, you maniac, you! Unbahleevabul! Get up there, guy! Get up there!

Fernando was confused. Everyone was clapping. They were all smiling and looking at him. He rose, tugged on the brim of his grimy Mets cap, and smiled back. Some teeth were missing. He scratched his mustache and put his hands in the pockets of his stained old army jacket.

— Go on, Fernando! commanded Monaghan.

He started to walk. He walked by McKenna.

McKenna slapped him on the back. He walked by Monaghan and he, too, slapped him on the back. Jimmy Santos smiled as Fernando passed. Franklin Henry clapped for him.

— Yay, Fernando! cheered Una as he smiled at her friend, Kathleen, and her.

Everyone was clapping, clapping, clapping. Mary stood aside from the table where the food had been to reveal a large basket wrapped in shiny plastic. Fernando peered through the plastic to see the many bottles of liquor and wine.

— There you are now, Fernando, congratulated Mr. Roach. You are this year's winner of the Basket of Cheer.

Staten Island, Manhattan 1991.

A Tragic Story
by Sister Beatrice Mahon, O.P.

Although Saint Joseph's Preparatory School in Philadelphia accepts only persons of the male gender, I have had, since my childhood, an abiding affection for that noble institution. I suppose that the seed of this affection was partially sown by several male members' of my family having attended the Prep. This supposition, however, is unsatisfying. It fails to articulate the root cause of my heart's sincere empathy for all the school's endeavors. I remember myself as a young woman cheering on its football and crew teams from the sideline and the riverbank. I fondly recall accompanying Preppers to their dances. To this day I thrill to the sound of men's voices singing, "Swing on along with the Crimson! Swing on along with the Grey," the opening lines of the Prep's fight song. I often ask myself why I have such fondness for a school that I did not attend and that, in fact, my sisters and I were unable to attend. Perhaps the best reason is this: I have watched, with steadily growing admiration for the Jesuit educators, my three brothers enter the Prep as boys and depart from those hallowed halls, as two of my uncles and a cousin had, as men. Since that time my admiration has intensified as I, myself, now a Dominican Sister, am laboring to educate the young women of Saint Thomas Aquinas High School in the Bronx and am sharing that experience with a fine dedicated alumnus of Saint Joseph's Prep.

The Reverend Pedro Arrupe, S.J., the Superior

General of the Society of Jesus, also known as "The Black Pope," once wrote that the goal of Jesuit education is the development of "men for others." Over the years, I have found that many Jesuit preparatory schools, colleges, and universities have been most successful in the development of persons for others. St. Joseph's Preparatory School, however, in my experience, seems to have been particularly blessed with the grace needed to develop such persons. I am thankful that I have had the opportunity to make acquaintances, friendships, and working relationships with so many of the Prep's idealistic and hard-working persons for others in both my hometown of Philadelphia and my present place of service, the Bronx. It is truly a blessing to have encountered so many Prep alumni providing a variety of services to "those in need."

A fine example of the type of person I am attempting to describe is Mr. Michael Mulligan. Mr. Mulligan teaches Global Studies and American Literature at Aquinas High School in the Bronx. He is as committed a teacher as I have ever been blessed with whom to have come in contact. He prepares and executes his lessons very well as evidenced by the success of his students. He is a gentle, patient educator as well as a firm disciplinarian.

He often telephones a student and her mother when a young woman has difficulty with whatever he might be instructing her in. Mr. Mulligan is also active in extra-curricular activities with our young women. He does fine work coaching our soccer team and assisting our softball coach. I have never known him to pass up an opportunity to spend extra time with a student-athlete. His popularity is nearly unanimous. If one walks the halls of our school with this Prep alumnus, this fact is made self-evident. "Hello, Mr. Mulligan," you will hear the young women all cry.

Even more extraordinary than the exemplary work which Mr. Mulligan does are his bearing and his demeanor, which I would describe (and please excuse my hyperbole as I am a mere educator in the service of God and not a literary artist) as, "saintly." I can find no other word that both denotes and connotes the impression of him that exists in my mind. His face exudes a radiance that I have seen in few others. His movements reflect the grace and dignity, the meekness and humility of a true saint. His conversation nearly always has as its theme our students and our school. In short, Mr. Michael Mulligan exhibits those qualities of the type of person about whom Superior General Pedro Arrupe S.J. has written and those qualities, having been instilled in him by the educators at St. Joseph's Preparatory School, have, in turn, been a force in our school and have caused me to apply the aforementioned adjective, normally reserved for the faithful departed, to the impression he has made upon myself and others. Mr. Mulligan lives the principles he has been taught. Because of this I here pay him my respects. He, unlike many less fortunate human beings, is at peace.

Mr. Mulligan has been endowed with the ability to personify the qualities that are most admirable among former Preppers. As much as I continue to admire him and those like him, however, I am disturbed by a recent experience I have had with a Prep alumnus. Over the Thanksgiving holiday this year I had a rather eye-opening encounter with a Prep graduate that has led me to conclude that my generalizations about the idealism of those whom St. Joseph's Prep sends out into the world need to be reevaluated.

My brother Brendan, his spouse, Kathleen, and their lovely little Brigid treated me to a splendid Thanksgiving in the true sense of the word. My work with the poor and disadvantaged in the Bronx has given me a real appreciation for this American tradition. Myself and my family have so much for which to be thankful, so many blessings which we need to recall and for which we need to be truly grateful in those quiet times when we put ourselves in the presence of God and we allow Him to come into our hearts, especially when one sees and works with those who have not been equally blessed and when one compares oneself with those hearty pioneers who ardently gave thanks to their Creator, Provider, and Savior after having survived that first winter in their newly found home in Massachusetts. Before our meal, Brendan, Kathleen, Brigid, and I attended mass at Saint Bernadette's Church in Drexel Hill, Pennsylvania. What a joy it was to watch young Brigid, that young white soul so close to God, carry the homemade bread her father had baked up to the altar to be blessed! Her attitude was not unlike that of the statue of the young Saint Bernadette kneeling before Our Lady outside of the church. I couldn't help but be moved by that lovely piety. Afterwards, I must confess, I indulged in a gluttonous second helping of turkey. (Soon the young women at Aquinas will be calling me *La Gordita*!)

The Friday evening after Thanksgiving has traditionally been set aside for the Homecoming Dance of St. Joseph's Preparatory School. I had not planned to go. Normally I do not attend such gala social events. However, I allowed my brother to easily talk me into joining him in revisiting his *alma mater.* With a mixture of apprehension due to my being unaccustomed to such events and a strange kind of excited anticipation the like of which I cannot recall as having had for some time, I left for the school for which I have felt so much admiration for as long as I can remember.

In the past, Saint Joseph's Prep has entertained its students, parents, alumni, and friends in Philadelphia's fashionable Center City hotels. During my youth the affair was held perennially at the well-known Bellevue Stratford. This hotel with its Old World elegance is inextricably tied to the memories of my young womanhood, of the Homecoming Dance and of SJP itself. (Of course, these were the days before Legionnaires' disease.) Other hotels have hosted the Preppers *et alia* since then but no venue has been able to replace the Bellevue in my mind and heart and in the minds and hearts of many others. This year the Prep tested out a new facility for its annual soiree — itself! SJP opened its doors on Friday night, November 26th to welcome home "The Prep Family." This made my coming home even more significant and disturbing than I would have anticipated. I was to socialize with old friends and acquaintances in the very hallowed halls of the Prep! Also, I was to see the contrast between the opulence of those halls and the devastation of the surrounding ghettoes of North Philadelphia. Although I must say the devastation pales in comparison with that of the South Bronx, I was, nevertheless, moved by reflecting on the lives of the poor, marginalized people who live in the rundown, three-story rowhouses by which we drove. I experienced some guilt over the fact that I was going to enjoy the company of the wealthy, the educated, the gay, in the midst of such poverty, ignorance, and despair. My mind entertained a notion of what it would have been like to throw open the doors of St Joe's Prep in a magnanimous gesture of personhood for others to the poor of North Philly but then thought better of this bit of whimsy. The poor will always be with us, I remembered. I did pray for them, though, silently, as my brother and Kathleen chatted over the chattering disc jockey and his rock and roll Hot Hits. The guilt did not leave me readily. It clung to me and cast doubts upon my soul as to whether my going to the Homecoming was right. After all, hadn't I just enjoyed a simple Thanksgiving during which I thanked God for all I have and prayed for those who are less fortunate? Now I was about to enjoy festivities that could be called nothing less than decadent while surrounded by the homes of the destitute. Still, this school, despite the inequity of material goods it and its beneficiaries possessed, had produced Michael Mulligan and countless other persons for others like him. Perhaps what did not make sense to my feeble mind was somehow reconciled in the Mind of the Divine. Besides, I couldn't very well have gotten out of the car and gone home alone, especially from that neighborhood. For the moment, I abandoned my feelings of culpability and allowed myself to celebrate the blessings of the good people with whom I was about to be surrounded.

As we climbed the stairs leading to the main entrance of the school, I was struck by the school shield displayed above the doors. It is the Prep's "coat of arms," if you will. The upper left quadrant shows the stripes of the House of Loyola. Two wolves sharing a cauldron of food are depicted in the upper right quadrant, representing hospitality (a fitting quadrant for this particular evening, I thought.) In the lower left quadrant is the lily of Saint Joseph, symbol of purity. The lower right quadrant contains a radiant circle inside of which are the Greek capital letters *Iota*, *Eta*, and *Sigma*, the first three letters of the name of Our Lord and Savior in Greek. Above these letters and inside the radiant circle is a cross, and, below the letters, still inside the round enclosure, are three nails. These are to remind us of the suffering of Our Lord because of our sins. This last quadrant is the symbol of the Society of Jesus. Below the arms are the initials of the Jesuit motto, A.M.D.G. (*Ad Maiorem Dei Gloriam*, For the Greater Glory of God.) These are wonderful arms and motto in my opinion. The seal calls to mind the great Spanish founder of the Society of Jesus, Saint Ignatius de Loyola, reminds us of our Christian duty to give and share as persons for others, calls us to be pure and chaste, and reminds us of the suffering, death, and resurrection of Christ which is the cornerstone of our faith and which, I believe, has inspired many of the young men who have crossed through the very same portal that I was then crossing to become persons for others. I thought of Michael Mulligan, a young lad of fourteen years, looking smart, perhaps, in a new suit and tie given him by his parents, entering this building for the first time and wondered how many other fine Catholic young men were inspired to live lives of service by Saint Joseph's Preparatory School.

At any rate, the atmosphere inside was quite festive. I imagine that anyone who did not have the holiday spirit before entering the Prep on that night quickly got in the mood of the season when that person arrived inside the Prep. The tapping of stepping dress shoes, the quiet murmur of casual conversation, occasional outbursts of hearty laughter, and faint, distant Big Band music were the sounds that greeted my ears upon entering. Men and women appropriately bedecked for the occasion stood in pairs and in larger groups conversing and sipping from their drinks. The foyer was beautifully decorated with illuminated Christmas trees surrounded by a myriad of gaily-decorated boxes of every size.

My brother politely offered to get drinks for the three of us and disappeared. I surveyed the foyer and glanced up toward the second and third floor galleries. I then turned my gaze toward the groups of young people. I tried to imagine myself in the place of the youthful and beautiful high school young women who wore corsages or carried roses given them by amorous young men from the Prep. Oh, to be in one of their places, to feel the first stirrings of nubile young womanhood rushing through me as if in celebration of God's nature, and to wear lipstick, makeup, carefully selected lacy undergarments, dresses, and jewelry, to receive and wear flowers to enhance my appearance and symbolize beauty, fertility, and the awakening of the spiritual and physical capacity for love! Oh, to be in that first flowering, that radiant evanescent flowering I had witnessed (and envied) so often in my students at Aquinas! Oh, how wonderful each young woman around me must feel, I thought, to be young, attractive, and in the arms of a Prepper!

"This is nice," remarked my sister-in-law.

I concurred, and, realizing that in my self-indulgent

reverie I had neglected Kathleen, I proceeded to make small talk with her about the pleasing decorations (hoping all the while that my face had not gotten flushed.) As I spoke with her, other thoughts occurred to me. Seeing beneath the glitter and color of the appearance of the place, as I am wont to do with places as well as with people, I saw a beauty that was modern and sterile. This was the "new Prep," the Prep of cubicle design, restrained sculpture, and glass. It was not the grandiose, classical, marble Prep that existed before the 1969 fire. No, this was the Prep that had foregone its heavy emphasis on classical studies for the more practical and mechanical computer age.

Brendan returned, drinks in hand, and escorted us past the gift boxes and Christmas trees, through the circles of Homecomers, and into the Multi-purpose Room. The gift box decor carried over into this room where adults spun around on the dance floor accompanied by an orchestra. We stood a bit awkwardly for a few moments and watched the dancers and the musicians. Our eyes scanned the gathering for familiar faces but found none immediately. My brother searched his pockets first for cigarettes and then for matches. Kathleen leaned most of her weight on her right foot and then shifted it onto her left. She took a cigarette and extended her neck toward Brendan who had offered her a lit match. I remained still. At that moment, I realized that I was the sole still person in the auditorium. Everyone else seemed to be in motion of one kind or another whether it was fidgeting, shaking hands, finishing drinks, throwing a head back in laughter, or twirling around the floor with a partner. Out of the whole assembly of adults of different ages, statures, and stations in life, I alone was still. This seemed somehow meaningful. However, I hadn't much time to ruminate over it as Brendan began introducing me to a former teammate of his.

"Beatrice, this is an old football buddy o' mine, Ironhead Whalen. Ironhead, this is my sister who's a sister, Beatrice."

"Hello, Mr. Whalen."

"Hello, Sister."

Launching into a conversation about the old football days, the two men swiftly sequestered themselves from us both physically and mentally. Kathleen decided that she and I would "visit the little girls' room," as she put it, and we were off down the hall in the direction of the gymnasium. I felt thankful for the opportunity to observe the young couples again. After using the Women's room, we wandered into the gym where the students and their guests "did their things" to the rock and roll music of a disc jockey. Kathleen momentarily wanted another drink and so we returned to her husband. We found him already in line to "purchase more refreshments" for the three of us.

"Nothing for me, Brendan," I said. "I'm quite satisfied for now."

Still sipping on my first Chardonnay, I took pleasure in the get together for another hour while renewing many old friendships and acquaintances. I met many men and women, both lay and religious, who were involved in doing fine work for others. Some of those who had not been called to the religious life were involved in their parishes, Catholic Youth Organizations, and other such non-profit groups, while others seemed to be happily answering a marital and familial vocation, which was quite heartening for me. In any case, all of those with whom I spoke at any length were persons for others whether those others were members of the world at large or members of the microcosm of that world, the family.

Now, the time has come, following these rather self-indulgent introductory remarks, for me to relate the story that contains the point of my writing. It was close to ten o'clock, as I recall, when I decided to buy a round of drinks. After a great deal of protestation from my brother, which, of course, was ineffectual, I joined the line of thirsty spirit purchasers. Two beverage buyers in front of me was a tall balding man in a charcoal grey suit. He had what I observed as a "Celtic" complexion, that is, pale, freckled or formerly freckled. (This type of skin is rare in the section of the Bronx with which I deal. Only some of my fellow teachers, the Sisters with whom I live, and some of the priests and brothers and police officers that I see have this type of complexion.) He wore a wedding band of considerable width and a rather ostentatious watch. His shoes, as far as my lack of expertise allows me to judge, seemed to be very expensive and the latest in style. I was somewhat surprised at myself for observing his appearance so closely. Normally, I pay little heed to externals. However, Providence must have directed my gaze toward him. The encounter was to prove most interesting, albeit disconcerting, for me.

All of those lined up to procure refreshments stepped forward as another customer had completed his or her transaction. Everyone in the line, with the exception of the man I had observed, waited patiently. The rest of the crowd chatted, chortled, or shrieked and hugged in reunion. They were smiling and moving. I, of course, was still. The man with the fashionable shoes and the ostentatious watch moved but he did not seem the smiling type. When the line shifted again toward the bartender, the blue-clad Celt collided with a clumsy (or tipsy) woman who spilled her drink down the front of him. He uttered a shocking oath.

"Jesus Christ!" he screamed.

Certainly I had heard far worse in the Bronx (and in Philadelphia, for that matter.) Still, I was shocked. Looking back, I see that this shock must have stemmed from my erroneous and unconscious belief that I was on hallowed ground, a ground free from incivility and blasphemy. I was indeed taken aback not only by this collision and subsequent outburst but also by the following exchange, which I give here to the best of my imperfect recollection as it has been some time since the occurrence and my mind has been occupied with my teaching duties in the interim.

"Why don't you watch where you're goin', lady?"

"I'm awfully sorry, sir. Here … here's a napkin. Uh … I'll go get some more."

"Don't bother," he rebuked. "You've done enough damage already! Do you know how much this suit costs?"

"I'm awfully sorry, sir."

The woman fled meekly yet swiftly away from this barbarous verbal assault. I felt pity for her and a good deal of anger over the man's treatment of her. I had half a mind to buy her a new drink and to offer him no consolation whatsoever. (I don't like to encourage that sort of thing, however. Besides, she seemed to have had a few already.) He had treated the poor woman like a second-class citizen and had embarrassed her publicly for an unfortunate mishap. It was uncalled for!

The man in the dampened suit mistakenly reacted as

if all of the eyes of the gathering were upon him. He returned his gaze to the bartender quickly, stubbornly, and, as it seemed to me, in an unnatural fashion. A moment later, presumably to relieve his embarrassment, the man tried to form an alliance with the male customer behind him, who, I assumed, was a stranger to him.

"Doesn't appreciate the price of anything," I heard him say. "Probably thinks it all grows on trees."

The listener said nothing.

"The irresponsible, clumsy," the man with the wet clothes continued, before adding with the furious intensity of one whose mouth is hurling the most vile of insults. "Woman!"

His intended audience smiled uncomfortably and again said nothing. I remained silent as well. Although I felt intensely my disapproval of his action, I did not act upon it. I preserved my aforementioned stillness. My heart, however, filled with indignant, righteous rage as well as with pity for the vanished, maligned woman. I had a powerful urge to purge this North Philadelphia temple of this money changer, but, as we moved toward the bartender once more, I noticed another and a rather surprising emotion welling up within me. It was embarrassment, not for the ill-treated woman but for the apparently socially clumsy and miserable man. It was the sort of embarrassment that is usually evoked by the foolish behavior of someone you know. I realized this immediately and also recognized its incongruity with the situation. I failed, therefore, to understand whence it sprung except if it were from the Holy Spirit guiding me to empathize with a person toward whom I was naturally inclined to feel contempt. If this were the case, I thought, then I was truly grateful for it, regardless of my poor comprehension of it.

I don't remember what it was — a turn of the head, a familiar step, a rubbing of the nose, a playing with change in a trouser pocket — that enabled me to recognize him. Nonetheless, suddenly, and with a potent mixture of delight and horror, I saw that it was Jimmy Walsh! It certainly seemed so, anyway, although I did have my doubts for an instant. It was as though I didn't want to believe what my senses were telling me. I thought to myself, "Could this really have been Jimmy Walsh; the Jimmy Walsh I had known to speak of nothing but basketball and Latin and Greek homework? Could that boy with whom I had once danced at the Bellevue Stratford have truly turned out to be the awful man that I had just seen so mistreat a woman for a simple and honest mistake?" Just then he paid for his drink and turned from the bar. All doubt vanished. It was he.

Jimmy was the son of Mr. John "Jack" Walsh, successful stockbroker, Villanova resident, member of the Overbrook Country Club and husband of a high school girlfriend of my mother. Mr. and Mrs. Walsh lived in their spacious Main Line home with their six children. John was the eldest followed by three sisters, Rose, Mary Kate, and Susan. Jimmy came next and his sister, Jacqueline, trailed closely behind him. My mother and Mrs. Walsh maintained their friendship with increasingly rare visits throughout their adult lives.

Due to the decreased frequency of these visits, I surmised, as I approached womanhood, that the friendship had become quite superficial, little more than an old habit. It seemed that socio-economic differences between Mrs.

Walsh, the wife of a wealthy stockbroker, and my mother, the wife of a moderately successful manager of a small supermarket in Lansdowne, had caused this. Hobnobbing at the Club and long evenings around an expensively set dinner table in Villanova held little appeal for my mother. The Donegal Ball and the other ceilis and dinner-dances at the Irish Center did not interest Mrs. Walsh. However, this is little more than pure speculation. There may have been no rift between them or that rift may have been a chasm for all I know for certain. I do know, nevertheless, that our family's visits to the Walsh homes in Villanova and Sea Isle City became fewer and farther between as the years passed and this is the cause to which I have always attributed this seeming estrangement.

It was during the years of this real or imagined increasing estrangement that I received a delightful phone call from a very shy Prep Junior. Jimmy wanted to know if I would go to the Prep's Homecoming Dance with him. I accepted at once. My heart raced with anticipation as the Thanksgiving holidays approached. I recall his gangly frame self-consciously trying not to stride ahead of mine as we walked to his father's car, his inhibited attempts at conversation and the long intervals of silence between them, his awkward movements on the dance floor (always keeping his body a more than respectable distance from mine), and his nervous mannerisms. I don't know whether it was because I was a friend of the family or whether it was because of some adolescent gynophobia, but he didn't even manage to call forth enough pluck to kiss me goodnight. It is not that I minded, though. In fact, I found all of these things — his self-consciousness, his inhibitions, his awkwardness, his nervousness, and his lack of presumption — to be quite charming. I was even charmed by his talk of Latin class, his lack of mastery of Trigonometry, caddying, and basketball, basketball, basketball. It seemed to me that he was doing all of the right things and that he would reach his career goal of journalism easily by remaining on the academic path on which he had already begun to tread, that he would surely turn out to be a true product of Saint Joseph's Prep. I had a vague hope that he would ask me for another date. He did not. Who knows what would have happened had he done so? We did remain friends, nevertheless, and kept in contact with occasional phone calls. After high school we lost touch and since graduation, I have carried with me the memory of him as an idealistic, awkward, basketball-dribbling St. Joseph's Prep student possessing a shyness whose charm was disarming and who was on his way to becoming a journalist of integrity. What a contrast that image was to the man he had become, to the man to whom I felt obligated to speak last November 26th.

My life, as one might imagine, is not exactly filled with intrigue. This, coupled with my years of controlled and direct body movement, made it difficult, if not unlikely, for me to observe Jimmy without his noticing me. His bright yellow tie with small lavender polka dots caught my eye at once. This I conjectured was what is known as a "power tie." I also took notice of how age had transfigured my friend. The brown, short-cropped, but full head of hair of my memory had since receded markedly. The steel-blue eyes that had once had the luster of innocence now seemed dull, hollow, and cold. They were even a little bloodshot. His face looked as if the intervening years since that high school dance had tired it. There were rings under his eyes and crows' feet marked the area around them. The signs of burst capillaries showed themselves near and on his nose. His posture seemed poor. His former flat athlete's stomach was now a paunch and his old cute habits were now robotlike, repetition having frozen them into a mechanical meaninglessness and charmlessness. I watched him fix his tie, sip his drink, pull up his trousers, all with the mechanical efficiency of a middle-aged man who is used to being watched by subordinates. I knew that he had spotted me. It was perhaps most obvious that I am a Nun. My posture, my short hair, my patient stillness were most likely in sharp contrast with the laity surrounding me. I wondered if Jimmy had grown so cynical (the look of him having caused me to deduce that cynicism was present within him) that he would think that I, a Sister, would have been staring at him with sexual interests in mind. I hoped not.

It seemed utterly unlikely that Jimmy would make the first move (as it had been at that other Homecoming some twenty odd years before) and just as unlikely that his conversation would prove scintillating. Therefore, (and nevertheless,) I moved toward him with outward control and inner misgivings, just as I have so often done in my teaching years since taking my vows. I sidled up next to him as he slapped the back of a departing "pal," smiled, and awaited an opportunity to speak.

"Excuse me, sir," I began, hoping to affect a comic bit of sarcasm in my tone of voice. "I believe we have some 'catching up' to do."

"Huh?" Mr. Walsh replied confusedly.

"Aren't you Jimmy Walsh?"

"Yeah. Well, yes. Uh … oh my God!"

I struggled to keep from cringing, as I feared a hearty slap on the back while my identity slowly dawned on him.

"Bea! How are you? I can't believe it! It's Bea Mahon!"

"Sister Bea Mahon now, Mr. Walsh."

I wasn't surprised when he suddenly grew less chummy. There was a falseness to his quasi-enthusiastic greeting that I knew he wouldn't have been able to keep up for long. His feigned cheerfulness disappeared from his face for an instant.

"Well, Sister, I certainly meant no disrespect. I-"

The phony, hail-fellow-well-met expression returned with remarkable speed (and resemblance to a genuine one), as I recall.

"How are you?" he cried.

I half-expected him to call me "pal" and I again had to restrain a cringe in anticipation of a backslap. Of course, the slap was not forthcoming.

"I'm doing well, thank you," I replied.

"What are you do- What brings you here, Sister?"

"Please, … call me 'Bea.'"

"O.K., what brings you here, Bea?"

Again his false smile was amazingly true to life. He continued.

"I have to admit it seems strange to call a Sister by her first name. You know us Catholic school boys never change."

"Oh, but we're old friends, Jim," I consoled.

There was an uncomfortable silence. I followed it with an answer to his question.

"I came here with my brother. You remember Brendan! I came here with his wife, Kathleen, and him. He talked me into it but I must say he didn't really have to twist my arm. So, how are you, Jim?"

"Oh, fine. Fine."

"I see you are wearing a wedding band."

"Oh, yeah. I've been married almost ten years now. I notice you're not wearing a habit."

"No. Well, we Dominicans haven't had to for some time now."

"Things sure've changed since we were kids — huh?"

"Certainly."

There was another silent pause.

"Is your wife with you tonight? I'd love to meet her," I said.

"No, no," he answered. "She had to fly out to London this morning for some kind of conference."

He seemed displeased by this as if his wife were a child undertaking a frivolous project or going through an annoying stage of development that he simply had to humor. I also noticed that, as we spoke, he twisted his body in odd ways. Later, I realized that he must have been attempting to conceal the wet spots on his clothing from my sight.

"I see. Well, it' s a pity that I'm unable to meet her."

"Yes. It could mean a promotion for her, though, and we could use the extra income. The little one, Beth, is in Montessori School, you know."

"How wonderful for you!" I exclaimed. "I'm so happy for you, Jim. She must be a wonderful child."

"Yes, yes, beautiful little girl. I'd like to spend more time with her, of course, but, you know how it is. I'm always on the run."

"What do you do?" I queried.

"I'm a broker for Kidder Peabody."

"Isn't that your fath-?"

"Yeah, same company," he interrupted. "But I … uh. … got the job on my own. No strings were pulled by the old man, believe you me."

The last part seemed like part of a well-rehearsed speech and I didn't believe him. Quickly, I recalled how one could never get the straight truth from Jimmy or from any of the Walshes. There was always this sort of uppercrust falseness to them. In Jimmy this falseness always had a certain innocence like the child who unwittingly repeats an untoward remark he or she had overheard at the dinner table. This was yet another quality which I found strangely endearing about Jimmy Walsh. I immediately saw that Jimmy had not lost his tendency to try to deceive nor had his attempts to deceive lost their transparent quality. However, this trait was not endearing as it once was. It had become pitiable. I could see the insane round of money chasing that his life had become. My mind envisioned his past — a rather immature college boy who played and fooled until graduation, never really pursuing his goal with any fervor, who continued playing and drifting for a few years more, after which his father decided that his son's irresponsible days were over and that if Jimmy weren't going to take control of his destiny, then he, the old man, certainly would. Somewhere along the line a wife and daughter appeared but I was sure Jimmy had been just as unconscious of these occurrences as he had been of his youthful malfeasance and his father's manipulation. I was saddened. I also had become distracted and at a loss for what to say next. Jimmy seemed to have run out of patience with having had to talk with a former date who had become a Nun and he also fell silent. Thankfully, as often happens at such moments, another "pal" slapped Jim on the back and engaged him in still more small talk.

He took leave of me saying, "It was great seeing you again, Bea. Say 'Hi' to your family for me. We'll have to get together sometime."

"We will," I responded. "Indeed."

This conversation may not seem much of a climax to my admittedly verbose and unskilled narration nor may it seem to be much of a tragedy to some, if not many or most. However, to me, it is both a climax and a tragedy. If a climax is a point of high intensity in a story after which all else is simply *denouement*, then this conversation was a climax for me. After this rather remarkable exchange of small talk, during which the visitation of the Holy Spirit, in the form of a vision of Jimmy Walsh's growth from adolescence to middle age, made the factors which produced the abhorrent man with whom I spoke as clear as crystal, I was left very empty and feeling forlorn. I longed for the silence and seclusion of an empty chapel. There, I felt, I would be able to reflect upon and complete the falling action of the story of this unhappy reunion. If a climax is a kind of ending, in which sense I believe the word is often used, then I have chosen the proper word, for, this meeting with Mr. Walsh was, for all intents and purposes, the ending of our friendship. He is gone from me now and I write "gone" intending for it to be understood in the way that it is among the Irish, that is, as a euphemism for those deceased. The Jimmy Walsh of my past, of my imagination, and of my hope and trust in his potential for being a good man is dead and gone. As regards Jimmy Walsh himself, the man is spiritually dead. He has become a well-attired, well-appearing, expertly talking, whited sepulcher. He seems to have no love, no true personality, nor, indeed, any individuality in God's creation. One cannot recognize him as having any particular ethnic origin or as having been brought up Catholic. I was positive that religion no longer held a place in his life, unless it had been relegated to the role of tradition or even of simply a habit of attending services. One would be unable to distinguish James Walsh from any stockbroker, insurance salesman, banker, or other such member of the business rank and file who hustle to the trains during the rush hours in Philadelphia, New York, or any metropolis worldwide. In other words, he is practically non-existent and this is why I have used the aforementioned euphemism, normally reserved for the dead, in reference to Mr. James Walsh.

I consider this talk with Mr. Walsh a tragedy because, as I (and perhaps only I) was and am able to see plainly, it was a downfall brought about by faults in his own character. Had young Jimmy Walsh been able to stay within the guiding embrace of Holy Mother the Church, had he prayed for direction and used God's help to come to some understanding of who he was and where he was going, had he subsequently avoided the irresponsible behavior which had brought about his father's stern patriarchal molding, and had he himself not succumbed to the dull glittering of gold, then this tragedy would have been averted. I see this and feel this as a true tragedy, for, I have, through my seeking him out, questioning him, and through the gift of the Holy Spirit, seen, in the brightest possible light, what has occurred in the life of my former friend. If Jimmy Walsh had retained his religion and his internal fortitude, if he had attained some degree of self-knowledge, then I would not have suffered the tragedy of losing my friend, but, if he ever does regain or attain these things I am certain that, then, the story of his life will become a true tragedy for him.

Philadelphia 1990.

Happy Birthday, Jacky Mack

Nervously, Jacky Mack's feeble fingers struggled to knot his thin black tie. Yes, indeedee, today was the day. Today was Thursday — the day they celebrated. Jacky Mack had been looking forward to its arrival all week, as he had done every week since they had made The Plan. The waiting, however, was over. Today was the day. And, today was extra special. It was his turn. Yes, indeedee.

His palsied digits completed the knotting of his tie and turned next to arrange the several hairs of his head. He squinted into the dusty looking glass to see himself. His skin had shrunken, wrinkled, clinging to his skull with a desperate grip. His eyes were a faded blue surrounded with pinkish lines like cracks in an unbroken egg. The eyes blinked back at him. He struggled to ignore them so that he could concentrate on the state of his blurry appearance. Today he decided to clean his glasses. It was very important that everything be perfect.

— Not bad for an old timer!

He smiled like a sentimental drunk about to cry with joy. A warmth spread over his pencil-thin frame and its worn white covering. Yes, indeedee, today was the day.

He leaned on the railing as he hobbled down the green-carpeted stairs. The wife had fixed everything just right. There were three chairs at the table in the kitchen. There were three plates, three glasses, and three sets of knives and forks. Just to make sure, though, Jacky Mack needed to double check. He took his clipboard down from the top of the refrigerator and vaguely recalled the face of the man who had given it to him, his former boss. That was before Penn Fruit had gone bankrupt and Jacky had been laid off.

— For all the long hours you spent tediously taking inventory, here's a token of my gratitude, small as it may be, he said after work one day when the place was empty.

Just me and him. Special. I used to live in that place. Hell, I spent an eternity there!

He went to the pen drawer in the kitchen and removed a blue ballpoint with which he created a table for his inventory:

Knifes	Forks	Plates	Glasses	Chairs	Tables

The lines separating his columns were straight and neat. In this, he took great pride. Thus, fifteen years of devoted service had not been wasted. He knew that there should be three of each except for the flags and tables of which there was to be one of each.

— Damn that woman! She forgot the glasses! Do I have to do everything myself?

In a fit of rage, he flung the cabinet door open, clumsily knocking a Saint Brigid's cross off of its nail and onto the to the floor. He looked up at the old nail in the woodwork over the sink.

— That boy don't even know how to hammer a nail in straight. If you want anything done right, you gotta do it yerself.

The Saint Brigid's cross was a gift. His daughter had brought it back from Ireland years ago. Jacky Mack had never been to Ireland but he had heard that it was a magical and holy place. He remembered the white plastic bag with a shamrock on it and the words, "SHANNON DUTY FREE" in green. The cross was made of woven reeds from the river Shannon. It was beauteeful. He quickly scooped it up, kissed it, and hung it on the old nail, his hands dancing and shaking around the cross for a moment in case it might fall again.

He returned to the table, took up the clipboard, and realized a second time that that woman had forgotten the glasses! Stomping back to the open cabinet, he took the glasses down and set them on the table. After writing a large, looping numeral three under "Glasses" in his inventory, he checked his black, digital watch. It was 9:05. They were late again. You would never know that they used to be in the Service.

Jack read the certificate that told of his stint in the U.S. Army during the Second World War. They usually waited until you were dead to honor you in such a way. At this, his heart beat proudly. Forty years ago, he got out. Age twenty six. The certificate was a little crooked on the refrigerator and so he straightened it out, his hands performing another nervous, shaking dance as he made sure the certificate's top was even with the refrigerator door's. He stepped back and read the familiar words of the magnet.

God said it.
I believe it.
That's enough.

He and the wife had always thought it was good to have those things around to teach the kids morality.

— Where are dose guys?!

The Septa bus wheezed to a halt, depositing Bill on the corner. The elfin figure slowly returned his Senior Citizen's pass to the pocket of his coat and limped carefully along the icy sidewalk. Jumping around in every trench in Europe for a year and never seriously injured. Then a patch of unseen ice ambushes him right in front of his West Philadelphia home last year. It didn't bother him much, though. No one to dance with, anyway. Whenever people asked about the leg, he gave them his simple, amiable, half-smile, looked at them with his childlike blue eyes growing sightless, and that's what he said:

— No one to dance with anyway.

Bill tried to hurry — knowing full well the anxious nature of his friends when he was late — but there wasn't much point in it. His legs wouldn't cooperate. Plus, he couldn't afford another spill.

Once again down this crooked street, I go. Watch out for the ice. Jacky's turn today. Wonder why he still lives in this neighborhood. The kids are off somewhere lucky to pay their rent after the drugs and booze. When they finally get some slut pregnant, they'll get married. Probly not before. One block survived. I should get a ride next time. Sure as hell not gonna pay for a cab. Lousy sons of bitches chargin' too much! I got better things to do with my hard-earned money! One of the few ones left who earned it hard, too.

Bill breathed a prideful sigh and looked up toward the low-lying sun. Out of the corner of his eye, he saw a canine lightning charge. It threw everything at him — every bark and bit of energy it could muster. It rushed at him like a startled green soldier fresh from Basic —too scared of losing his own young life not to kill — baring its teeth and snarling, too eager for the action because he'd never seen it, until it reached the fence. And thank God for fences!

Another half a block and Bill reached the black door. It was opened almost before Bill could ring the bell.

— Willy! How dee doo? Jacky exclaimed with almost too much excitement. He offered his skeletal hand to his visitor but had to withdraw it as the hunched-over little man leaned on the railing to scale the three front steps to the Mack abode. Bill panted and unbuttoned his overcoat.

— I'm doin' all right, Captain. How's yerself?

— Jus' wunnerful, Willy. Jus' wunnerful. Lemme close dis door before we catch our death. It's a bit nippy — ain't it?

— Oh, it's bitter out there.

Bill held his heavy jacket in his unsteady hands and awkwardly looked for a place to put it.

— Here … Here, lemme take that, Bill. I'll put it upstairs in de bedroom. Here … gimme it.

— No, no, don't go to any trouble on my account. I'll do it.

— Don't even think it, Willy. Jacky yanked it from Bill's grasp and mounted the stairs as quickly as can be expected.

— I'll put on a fresh pot, shouted Bill to the second floor.

— Sidown, Willy. Yer a guest in my home!

— But I ain't a freeloader.

Bill smiled at his comeback and continued:

— If dere's one thing I ain't afraid of, it's hard work.

He disappeared into the kitchen.

A yellow cab maneuvered through the cars parked at odd angles and the unusual turns that Jacky Mack's street took and stopped in front of the house. Joe stepped out of the taxi, wearing a wide-brimmed hat and a long, tan trenchcoat, which made him look even shorter than he actually was. With a white Entenmann's box tucked under his left arm, Joe struggled to get out his wallet and give the driver his fare and a good tip. Then, taking the cigar out of his mouth, he thanked the man heartily.

— See ya next week! Joe promised.

— You know it! Thanks, Joe, the driver said and pulled away smiling.

Joe toddled between the parked cars and looked up at Jacky's house. It looked as if it were about to fall and knock the rest of the homes in its row down like dominoes. Standing on the sidewalk, he turned his head and contemplated the image, watching the houses falling down the steadily descending slope. His brown eyes twinkled with amusement and his swarthy cheeks jumped with a quick smile and puff on his cigar.

— Sorry I'm late, Jack. My wife, she's drivin' me nuts. Didn't want me comin' out in the cold and the ice. So I says, "All right. I'll take a cab if yih jus' shut up." I brought the Entenmann's.

Joe handed over the box. Upon receiving it, Jacky's face lit up like a Christmas tree. His eyes opened wide and blinked into it. His lips strained to smile wider than his wrinkled face seemed able to allow. Blushes and tears seemed to rise at the same instant, as if Joe's gift was too much to handle. It was a pound cake.

He was still staring at it when Bill shouted from the kitchen:

— Pot's boilin'! Come an' get it!

Jacky and Joe hurried toward the sound, the former taking the frantic lead and the latter waddling behind him. From the plastic sleeve on the counter, each took a styrofoam cup and waited for it to be filled. They were panting and impatient.

— Say, that's good, Bill, Joe congratulated. He shook Bill's hand.

The three stood and slurped their hot drinks until Bill, offering a cigarette to each of his companions, said:

— Here! Smoke 'em if yih got 'em!

Jacky took one and offered great thanks. Joe declined, still working on his cigar. After a few minutes of slurping and smoking, Jacky announced:

— Well, I guess it's about that time …

All at once the three began scurrying about the room, rearranging the furniture. They moved the potted plants. They shoved chairs and lifted tables. Jacky wrote down every completed task on his clipboard. They changed the locations of pictures on the walls and on the tables. They were a force in constant — albeit slow — motion for about 45 five minutes, after which time just about all of their energy was spent.

Jacky slapped the back of Joe who slapped the back of Bill. Bill slapped Joe and Jacky on the back and Joe slapped Jacky who then slapped Bill on the back. It was a job well done and now they were going to relax. After the festivities, they were going to follow Jacky's list and replace everything before she got home. But, now it was time to seat themselves around the table in the tiny kitchen. Jacky broke the seal of the Entenmann's box and began to say grace:

— Blessis, O Lord, and dese dy gifs …

After he gave thanks, he cut the cake and gave a piece to each of his friends.

— Y'know, we gotta keep doin' this every week.

— We have been, Jacky, countered Joe.

— I know dat but we gotta keep on rememberin'.

— We will, reassured Bill.

Then Jacky Mack took the bottle of milk and filled the three glasses, saying:

— Eat up! And drink up! This is my turn and I want everyone to enjoy themselves!

With that, the two friends lifted their glasses and exclaimed:

— Happy birthday, Jacky Mack!

Philadelphia 1985.

ABOUT BOANN BOOKS AND MEDIA LLC: Boann was the Irish goddess of poetic inspiration. According to Celtic legend, Boann removed the cover from a forbidden sacred well and released the waters of poetry and the Salmon of Knowledge into the world, thus creating and giving her name to Ireland's River Boyne. Boann Books and Media strives to publish and produce works of art: literary, theatrical, and cinematic. We embrace works that are innovative and experimental while cognizant of the timeless traditions of literature, theatre, mythmaking, and storytelling. We intend our multi-layered works to address the core of human experience. Like Boann, we seek to use unconventional means to bring something beautiful and powerful into the world. We hope that our works both reflect and engender inspiration. Visit **boannbooksandmedia.com**.

ABOUT THE AUTHOR: John Kearns grew up in the Philadelphia area, where he attended St. Joseph's Prep and St. Joseph's University. John has an MA in Irish Literature from the Catholic University of America and lives in Manhattan with his wife, Mei, and stepson, Wang Zhi. His novel, *The World*, was published in 2003. His novel in progress, *Worlds*, was a finalist in the 2002 New Century Writers' Awards. John has read from his own work in venues throughout New York City, Philadelphia, and Washington, DC, and has had several Off-off Broadway plays produced, including the full-length *Sons of Molly Maguire* (2007), *In a Bucket of Blood* (2006), and *Designers with Dirty Faces* (2005) and the one-act "The Importance of Loving Shakespeare" (1999, 2005), "World Piece" (2003), "I Knew You'd Say That!" (2005), the 8-Minute Madness finalist, "Hanging Questions" (2006), and "Copy 8852" (2007), a collaboration for the Ontological Theatre. Visit **kearnscafe.com**.

www.ingramcontent.com/pod-product-compliance
Lightning Source LLC
Chambersburg PA
CBHW031109260626
47172CB00001B/291